-BOOK THREE-

MIDNIGHT

AND THE PH

D0372348

-BOOK THREE-

MIDNIGHT REYNOLDS

AND THE PHANTOM CIRCUS

CATHERINE HOLT

ALBERT WHITMAN AND COMPANY
CHICAGO, ILLINOIS

WITHDRAWN

Library of Congress Cataloging-in-Publication data is on file with the publisher.

Text copyright © 2019 by Catherine Holt
Cover art copyright © 2019 by Ayesha Lopez
First published in the United States of America in 2019 by Albert Whitman & Company
ISBN 978-0-8075-5132-5 (paperback)
ISBN 978-0-8075-5133-2 (ebook)

All rights reserved. No part of this book may be reproduced or transmitted in any
form or by any means, electronic or mechanical, including photocopying,
recording, or by any information storage and retrieval system,
without permission in writing from the publisher.

Printed in the United States of America
10 9 8 7 6 5 4 3 2 1 LB 24 23 22 21 20 19

Design by Aphee Messer

For more information about Albert Whitman & Company,
visit our website at www.albertwhitman.com.

100 Years of Albert Whitman & Company
Celebrate with us in 2019!

In memory of Marg Holt.
My sweetest of mother-in-laws.
You'll always be missed.—CH

CHAPTER ONE

"Get me out of here!" a voice cried out.

A bone-chilling scream split through the air as a flash of green light illuminated the low-pitched ceiling and closed-in walls. Dangling cobwebs covered every surface.

Midnight Reynolds swallowed as skeletal fingers brushed along her skin. Then the room filled with eerie laughter, and someone else started wailing in terror. The voices around her were still screaming several minutes later when the Amazing House of Horrors Ghost Ride finally lumbered out of the dark chamber and back into the daylight before coming to a shuddering halt.

The skinny guy who'd been operating the controls jumped down from the booth and opened the gleaming silver doors of the cars.

"That's it, folks. Hope you enjoyed the ride, and don't forget to come back again. Unless you're too scared," he added in a low, gravelly voice, which caused a couple of nearby girls to squeal in protest.

"Scared? Please." Midnight's best friend, Tabitha, snorted as she climbed out of the car to exit the Amazing House of Horrors. "I've been on hayrides that were creepier."

"And ghosts don't actually wear white sheets with eyeholes in them," Midnight said as she took out a tissue to clean her glasses. They were wire-rimmed, and, when combined with her brown hair, they made her look like a goblin. But when she wore them, she really could see ghosts.

To be more precise, she could see spectral energy—tiny snowflake-like fragments that were the souls of the dead. It was a rare gift that had developed nine months ago when she'd turned twelve (at midnight on Halloween). At first she'd been terrified, but in time she learned more about her ability and how spectral energy worked.

For instance, it gathered in areas known as Black Streams before crossing over to the Afterglow. Spectral energy was good, except when it became trapped in inanimate objects. Then it turned into something dark and dangerous known as planodiume.

When planodiume fell into the wrong hands, it could cause untold amounts of harm. Which was why Midnight—the only person in Berry, West Virginia, who could see spectral energy—had been recruited by the Agency of Spectral Protection (ASP) to make sure planodiume wasn't being misused.

Midnight's friend Tabitha was still talking about the disappointing Amazing House of Horrors ride. "They could've used a lot more imagination. Their skeletons weren't even anatomically correct." Tabitha loved everything dark and gothic. When she'd first found out about Midnight's strange ability, she'd thought it was cool. Now she was working for the ASP too, putting her research skills to use.

"And the fake spiders weren't poisonous ones," Midnight added.

The two girls joined the milling crowds that had come

to see the traveling circus. It was a perfect summer day, and the bright-orange sun hung high in the sky, surrounded by marshmallow clouds. Excited chatter rose like helium balloons as people strolled by with their corn dogs and sodas, and the air was filled with the buttery scent of popcorn.

"What do you want to do before the show starts? And do *not* say 'visit Zelda the fortune-teller.'" Tabitha flicked the poker-straight ebony hair that fell down her back. To celebrate completing seventh grade last week, her friend had added several blue streaks, along with a nonpermanent skull tattoo on her arm.

"I wasn't going to." Midnight crossed her fingers as they walked past the tent where Zelda the Great was sitting. Zelda was decked in jewelry with a fringed scarf wrapped around her shoulders, while her pink lipstick stood out against her Day-Glo tan.

Okay, so she *was* going to suggest visiting Zelda.

Because if the fortune-teller really could see into the future, she might be able to help Midnight plan her summer break. Well, plan it more.

She was already organizing her time using a new specially designed color-coded spreadsheet. Red was for her job keeping spectral energy safe. Green was for hanging out with Tabitha and having fun. And pale yellow was for times Logan might have the chance to kiss her.

She needed help planning that last part.

After Midnight's older sister, Taylor, was kidnapped by her crazy, evil, planodiume-wielding boyfriend, Logan had helped save the day. Since then, he'd started working at ASP with Midnight and Tabitha. Even more exciting was that he and Midnight were now boyfriend and girlfriend.

But that had been two months ago, and they still hadn't locked lips. Tabitha said Midnight should just let herself be surprised, but she didn't agree. She had enough surprises with her work as a protector. In real life, she liked things to be planned and organized.

Plus, she'd already gone through three tubes of cherry lip gloss. Waiting to be surprised was expensive.

Tabitha nodded toward the fortune-teller's tent. "I bet if you went to Zelda, she'd just tell you the same thing she tells everyone. *'You're going to meet a stranger with blue eyes. Watch out for the number five, and whatever you do, don't choke when you eat pizza.'*"

"Is that so?" a familiar voice said from behind them. Tabitha let out an uncharacteristic squeal as Tyson Carl approached. They'd been dating for almost as long as Midnight and Logan, and despite seeming like the opposite of one another (Tyson was really into sports), they were turning out to be a perfect match.

"I thought we were meeting after the show." Tabitha frowned, trying to regain her cool.

"My fault," another voice said. It was Logan, closely followed by his three-year-old mini-me sister, Bella. "We were planning on doing the rides, but Mom wanted me to take Bella for an hour. Hey, Midnight."

"Hey," she replied, her face heating. Logan had rumpled brown hair, chocolate eyes, and a lopsided smile, and his olive skin had darkened with the fine weather.

I hope he doesn't know I was thinking about kissing him.

When they'd first met, she'd hardly been able to speak in full sentences around him, and even now she sometimes lost her train of thought. Though not when they were working. When spectral energy and bad guys were involved, she was totally fine. She just had problems with everyday situations.

Midnight self-consciously patted her denim shorts and favorite unicorn T-shirt and wondered whether she should've brushed her hair before putting it up in a ponytail.

"Look what I got." Bella thrust out a hideous rainbow-colored teddy bear that appeared to have been run over by a train. "Logan won it!"

"It's beautiful." Midnight crossed her fingers, while Tabitha made a choking noise.

"It would've been cheaper to take her to the toy store." Logan wrinkled his nose, but Bella didn't seem to notice as she carefully patted the pastel-colored fur of her prize.

Just then, a sharp, pinging noise rang out. Midnight, Tabitha, and Logan instantly pulled out the phone-like devices that the ASP had recently given them. Technically, they were called sonic detectors and were used to track and measure spectral energy, but Midnight and her friends had nicknamed them Pings, thanks to the short, sharp warning sound the devices made.

The three friends checked the screens of their Pings, but no warning messages flashed up. The high-pitched noise sounded again, and Tabitha let out a soft groan and pointed to the bear that Bella was still hugging. It had some kind of mechanism under the fur that played music.

A false alarm. Midnight, Tabitha, and Logan pocketed their devices again.

"Okay, so that was weird." Tyson frowned as he studied the three of them. Midnight winced. Part of their job was to be discreet. "Is there some secret club I should know about?"

"O-of course not," Tabitha quickly answered. "It's er…just a new music app we were trying out."

"Any good?" Tyson asked, retrieving his own phone, his eyes gleaming with interest. "Perhaps I should get it."

"Actually," Logan quickly cut in. "It's pretty bad. I'm about to delete it. It takes up way too much memory."

"Way too much," Tabitha parroted.

"Sure. At least tell me you've figured out a way to smuggle us into the VIP section of the show," he said, though a teasing note had returned to his voice. Midnight gave a mental sigh. That had been too close.

"Sorry." Tabitha shook her head. Her dad was the fire chief and had only managed to get two extra VIP tickets, which were for Midnight and Tabitha.

"Worth a try," Tyson said. "I guess we'll just have to slum it with Logan's folks."

"They're probably waiting for us," Logan said before coughing. "But Midnight, I was wondering if you wanted to go to the swimming pool on Wednesday. Um, and you can both come too. I mean, if you want to," he added, glancing at Tabitha and Tyson.

"Count me out. I'm staying with my grandma for a couple of days. I won't be back until Friday." Tyson shook his head.

"I'll pass." Tabitha held out a pale white arm with pride. "Sitting in the sun isn't my idea of a good time. That means it'll just be you two."

"Oh." Midnight's eyes widened. A whole day with just the two of them having fun sounded...amazing. She mentally moved things around in her spreadsheet to clear some room. "S-sure. I'd like that."

"Cool." Logan let out a breath and gave her a small smile as Bella tugged at his arm. "Okay, we'd better go, but we'll see you after the show so we can arrange it."

"Still want to see Zelda?" Tabitha grinned as her hair fell down around her shoulders like a curtain.

"Fine, so you were right. Sometimes *not* planning things is a good idea. Are you sure you didn't want to come?"

"One hundred and fifty percent sure. Besides, I'm planning a trip to the cemetery. They're restoring some of the old gravestones down by the river. I want to take photographs. I was going to invite you, but somehow I think you'd rather be at the pool."

"I can go if you want me to," Midnight said in an uncertain voice, but Tabitha just cut her off with a laugh.

"Relax. I'm joking. You and Logan will have a great time." She grinned, the blue streaks in her hair bright against the sun.

"You're the best."

"That's what friends are for." Tabitha shrugged, but Midnight wasn't fooled. Tabitha pretended that she didn't care what people thought of her, but she'd been ignored and bullied just as much as Midnight had for standing out and being different. Which was probably why neither of them took their friendship for granted. "Well, that and scoring VIP seats," she added as her phone beeped. "It's from my dad. He's ready to meet us."

"VIP seats, here we come." Midnight smiled as they

made their way to the large circus tent at the far end of the rides and attractions.

People of all ages were lined up, including several teachers from school, one of her stepfather's friends dressed up as a Viking, and the woman who owned the flower shop at the mall.

Not that Midnight was surprised. For the last two weeks, posters had been plastered all over town. The poster had a photograph of an old-fashioned ringmaster with black hair, a giant top hat, and a twirling mustache. In one hand was a coiled whip, and in the other was a megaphone.

Step right up!

Cirque Fantastic is here.

Our animal-free acts will leave you

Spellbound and Amazed!

Fairground Attractions and Rides Galore.

Come one, come all, to the most spectacular show on earth!

Two days ago, a procession of trucks and trailers had snaked into town, setting up on a large stretch of parkland. Soon the place was transformed into a city of amusement tents and rides with a giant big-top tent at one end.

"There he is," Tabitha said as a tall man with dark hair

waved them over. Mr. Wilson had a straight nose similar to Tabitha's. Despite the warm weather, he was wearing his thick, navy fire chief blazer with gold badges and a crisp white shirt and tie.

He greeted both the girls and nodded in the direction of the tent. "Come and meet Carlo De Rossi, the ringmaster."

"De Rossi?" Tabitha frowned. "Why do I know that name?"

"Because he's famous, and I'm a cool dad for introducing you?" Mr. Wilson suggested and quirked an eyebrow. Tabitha groaned in response.

"For starters, anyone who calls themselves 'a cool dad' isn't. And second, I remember why I know the name. There's a De Rossi headstone in the cemetery."

"Why am I not surprised?" The fire chief gave his daughter an affectionate smile. Though both her parents were more the sporty type, Tabitha preferred to wear black and spend her time researching the local cemetery. Mr. Wilson grinned. "Does that make me cool?"

"Still no," Tabitha assured him, but returned his smile as they reached a side entrance.

Midnight let out a gasp as they stepped inside the big top.

The circular floor glowed white, and towering poles entwined with purple lights stretched up to the striped roof, filling the entire place with a mauve glow. From the poles, wires spun out in all directions like an intricate spider's web. The tiered rows of seats around the outside of the ring were quickly filling with people, their phones flashing as they all took photos. To the left were the VIP seats, a row of plush velvet chairs, blocked off by a golden rope. Even Tabitha looked impressed.

A man came forward to greet them. He had jet-black hair, a hooked Roman nose, and heavy lids over his dark eyes, and he wore a bright-blue coat with long tails down the back and more golden badges and buttons than even the fire chief. On his head was a tall black hat, and his knee-high leather boots gleamed.

The ringmaster.

"John." He greeted Tabitha's father. "How did the final safety check go?"

"You're all clear, but I'm going to have a couple of guys on-site the entire time. You run a tight ship."

"Trust me, if this were a ship, I would've made a couple of people walk the plank," Carlo confided with a laugh.

Midnight widened her eyes, but if Mr. Wilson thought the comment was funny, he gave no sign of it. Instead he just smiled. "Carlo, I'd like you to meet my daughter, Tabitha, and her friend Midnight. They're excited to see the show."

"Nice to meet you both." Carlo flashed bright-white teeth and offered the girls a flourishing bow. He was obviously a born performer. "I hope you enjoy it. We've traveled all around America, but we haven't come back to Berry since the death of my great-great-grandfather many years ago."

"I knew it!" Tabitha grinned before seeming to notice the flicker of confusion in Carlo's eyes. She gave an apologetic cough. "Sorry. I've seen a gravestone in the cemetery for a De Rossi and figured you must be related."

"Ah! I'm proud to have the same blood as Eduardo De Rossi. His father, Antonio, started Cirque Fantastic but Eduardo made it truly spectacular. He was one of the greatest showmen in the world. There he is."

He pointed to the full-length picture on the wall, similar to the one on the posters around town. It was easy to see the two men were related. In fact, if it wasn't for the sports watch on Carlo's wrist, they could've been the same person.

"I'm sure you're doing a great job of carrying on in his footsteps," Tabitha's dad said.

"It's my reverent wish to make him proud." Carlo beamed. Just then, a solemn-looking clown with blue hair raced over and whispered something into the ringmaster's ear. "Please excuse me. We go on in five minutes, and I have some things to attend to." Then, with another flourishing bow, he jogged over to where a gymnast was having a heated argument with a woman holding several long, sharp knives.

"We'd better go find our seats." Mr. Wilson glanced at the roped-off area. The chairs were much nicer than in the tiered section, and Midnight and Tabitha grinned in approval. This was definitely the perfect way to start their summer vacation.

Midnight scanned the huge tent until she found Logan. She gave him a small smile as he held up the ugly bear Bella had won, using its paw to wave at her.

"Please tell me you're not going to be pulling goofy faces at him for the entire show," Tabitha muttered.

"I promise," Midnight said, though it wasn't her fault Logan was so adorable.

They sat down as the lights dimmed and the music that had been playing came to a halt. The buzz of conversation died away, and purple lights pulsed around the tent. A drumroll shattered the silence, and a spotlight flicked onto Carlo, who was standing in the center ring, surrounded by a circle of performers.

The crowd hollered in approval, and Midnight and Tabitha clapped their hands. Even Mr. Wilson let out an excited shout.

"Thank you!" Carlo called out to the audience. "In 1871, Antonio De Rossi started this circus right here in Berry. It was then taken over by his son, Eduardo—the man who made even Harry Houdini jealous with his amazing skills. I know both Antonio and Eduardo would be delighted that we've finally come home! Now, I have just one question for you. Are you ready for the greatest show the world's ever seen?"

"Yes," the crowd thundered back, so loud it seemed like the floor was shaking.

"I can't hear you." Carlo raised his arms in the air like a conductor.

This time, everyone stood and cheered as the ring-master gave a dramatic sweep of his hands and spurts of flames rose from the ground. They were accompanied by the *bang, bang, bang* of a drum as the performers stepped into action.

A gymnast ran around the ring doing cartwheels, while a pair of acrobats bounced up and down on the trampolines. There seemed to be something happening in every part of the stage. Then the ringmaster blew a whistle and the performers retreated, leaving only the knife-thrower and her terrified-looking assistant.

"Let the show begin," Carlo said as the woman threw a knife high in the air.

The metal blade flashed as it spun several times before she caught it by the handle. Then she gave the crowd a wolfish grin and began her act.

The next hour was a blur of excitement as one act after another came out, showing skills, flexibility, and stamina.

"This is pretty cool," Tabitha murmured as the blue-haired clown they'd seen earlier stepped into the ring.

His eyes and mouth were highlighted with dripping makeup, and a grotesque smile was painted onto his face. He was wearing an old checked suit with wide legs and a black-and-white shirt underneath.

He gave the audience a shy wave as he tripped and shuffled his way to a wooden platform not far from the VIP area. The audience laughed at his awkward progress.

The laughter increased as a burst of flames rose up from the ground, and the clown tumbled back in mock surprise. He righted himself and pretended to sniff the flames, much to the crowd's delight.

He picked up a baton from the ground and thrust it into the flames until it was lit. Then he fumbled and dropped the flaming baton before finally holding it high in the air.

"I think he's going to eat it." Midnight gulped as Mr. Wilson leaned forward in his chair. This was obviously one of the acts he'd been asked to check.

On cue, the clown lowered the flaming baton toward his face. The audience sucked in their collective breath as he did his fire-eating act, finally pulling the baton out of his mouth and grinning.

The big top erupted in applause, and he once again held the flaming baton in the air as he took a bow.

Midnight was about to clap when a low buzz rang in her ears. It was as if hundreds of bees had suddenly been let loose. Except she knew all too well there were no bees. Whenever she heard the noise, it meant only one thing.

Spectral energy was nearby.

Goose bumps traveled up her arm. If the energy was trapped for too long, it would turn into planodiume, and she was the only one who could stop it.

So much for a quiet summer. She jumped to her feet as a splinter of blinding light ripped through the big top. Whatever was about to happen, it wasn't good…

CHAPTER TWO

"Are you okay?" Tabitha asked, her eyes studying Midnight's face, trying to figure out what she was seeing.

"No." Midnight shook her head. "There's something wrong with—"

The buzzing increased, and jagged splinters of golden light ripped through the big top and speared straight down to the clown, engulfing him like a blazing halo. A silent scream caught in Midnight's throat as the blinding light darkened into a sickening black fog.

A sickening fog that only *she* could see.

Damp decay clogged her nostrils as tendrils of

darkness danced and swirled around the clown, glittering like obsidian.

Something sharp and sibilant hissed through the air and then snapped back, a violent cracking noise ringing out around the tent. She scanned the tent, but there was no sign of whatever had made the noise. Only the blank faces of the audience, unaware of the chaos happening all around them.

A shower of golden sparks mushroomed out across the ceiling. Then, as quickly as it had appeared, the raging fog swirled up through the spire at the center of the tent, as if being sucked out by a vacuum.

Midnight pressed her glasses farther up her nose. Usually planodiume only disappeared if she used one of her weapons to release it. So where had it gone?

"Something's wrong?" Tabitha's face drained of color. "Like what?"

The clown continued to wave, oblivious to what had just happened. But, as he turned to face the VIP area, she finally saw his eyes.

They were blazing with liquid gold, his mouth slack and his expression blank.

In the last nine months she'd seen a lot of crazy things.

Melting artifacts, flying ghost daggers, and an old woman who'd lived to be one hundred and fifty—all because of misused spectral energy. But she'd never seen anyone's eyes turned to gold before.

"It's some kind of spectral energy," Midnight told Tabitha. "But different—"

Before she could finish, the clown crumpled to the ground as if he were a puppet whose strings had been cut. The burning baton fell from his hand and the entire platform he'd been standing on erupted into flames, sending up rippling shades of orange and yellow heat.

The crowd was silent.

Mr. Wilson raced to the center of the ring and dragged the unconscious clown away from the fire. Two firemen appeared with extinguishers to put the flames out. They were joined by a team of medics carrying a stretcher and a large equipment bag.

Over the din, a panicked Carlo used a loudspeaker to reassure the audience everything was okay as ushers directed people out of the tent in an orderly fashion.

The arid stench of burning wood caught in Midnight's nose.

"What about my dad?" Tabitha's face was paler than normal as the ushers tried to lead them out.

"I'm fine, Tab. I promise." Mr. Wilson jogged over and put a reassuring hand on his daughter's arm. "Go outside. The boys have everything under control, but I need to assess what happened. I'll call your mom and Midnight's parents so they can pick you up. The circus is finished for the day."

"Okay." Tabitha nodded, and the pair of them followed the trail outside. Night had begun to fall, and crowds of people huddled together staring at the tent, the faint stench of smoke still hanging in the air.

The carnival music that'd been playing all day had been switched off, and the lights from the many rides and amusements had stopped flashing, leaving the place in eerie silence.

"I can't believe that just happened." Midnight shivered as people pushed past them, all heading in the direction of the parking lot.

"I don't even know *what* happened." Tabitha's voice was still shaky. "Did you see something?"

"P-planodiume," Midnight stammered. "But it was

different. The clown was covered in light. Then, before he collapsed, his eyes turned golden."

"I've never read about that happening. Was there anything else?"

Midnight nodded. "There was a noise. Like lightning or hissing energy, followed by a crack. Did you hear it?"

"No. And why weren't we notified?" Tabitha's brow furrowed, and she dragged her Ping out of her purse. Confusion flickered in her eyes. "There's no planodiume here. Whatever you saw has gone."

"But *where's* it gone?" Midnight closed her eyes and tried not to panic. It was hard. Because it was her job to find it before anyone else got hurt.

* * *

"Are you okay?" her mom asked an hour later as Midnight climbed into the restored 1955 Ford that her new step-father, Phil Lockwood, drove. Her mom and Phil had been at the movies, so Midnight had gone back with Tabitha until she could be picked up.

"Yeah. The firemen put the blaze out quickly." Midnight waved goodbye to Tabitha, who was standing at the front gate. And although she didn't speak, her look clearly said: *Call me as soon as you hear back from Peter Gallagher.*

Midnight nodded in silent acknowledgment as Phil pulled out onto the street. Peter Gallagher was the head of the Agency for Spectral Protection. He was also her boss, and she hoped he'd have some answers for her.

"Do they know how the fire happened?" Phil asked, his eyes ahead on the road. On the weekends he liked to dress up as a Viking, but during the week, he stuck to the present century, so he was wearing jeans and a T-shirt. Though, with his long beard and sideburns, he still looked to Midnight like a Viking.

"The torch the clown was holding fell onto the platform. But Mr. Wilson said it shouldn't have been enough for the platform to catch fire. That's why he closed the circus down to make sure everything's okay," Midnight said. But she wasn't so sure herself that everything was okay.

If the torch hadn't started the fire, did that mean planodiume had?

And where had the planodiume gone? In her experience, it didn't just disappear.

She leaned back against the seat. So many questions. So few answers.

"Such a pity," her mom said. "I was speaking to that lovely woman who runs the organic store, and she told me this is the first time Cirque Fantastic has visited Berry in over a century. I hope they don't take this fire as a bad sign."

"I'm sure that won't happen." Phil turned right at the lights. "John Wilson's a first-class fire chief. He'll get to the bottom of this, and then it'll be business as usual."

"I hope so," her mom said. Midnight wasn't sure she agreed. Of course she wanted the circus to be open so she could enjoy it. After all, she was on her summer break. But if someone *was* misusing planodiume, it would be safer for everyone if the circus was shut down.

Midnight looked out the window of the Ford. Why were they going past their turnoff? She furrowed her brow as Phil took another right and then pulled into the parking lot of Cookies and Cakes.

The café had opened just after Christmas, and she'd taken to thinking of it as her and Logan's place. They'd been there ten times now—and yes, she might've tracked those visits in her spreadsheet.

Each time, they'd sat in the corner booth splitting a brownie and talking about their favorite books. It had also been where he'd officially asked her to be his girl-friend. She could still see his smile, and the way his eyes had nervously scanned her face when he'd asked her. As if unsure of how she was going to answer. It had been one of the greatest days of her life.

Then she frowned. It might be her happy place, but it wasn't somewhere her vegan mom ever came to.

In fact, it was the polar opposite to the vegan café her mom was in the process of setting up. Something was fishy.

Midnight leaned forward and stared at the back of her mom's head. "What's going on? Why are we here?"

"No reason," her mom said as Phil switched off the engine. "We just thought it would be a nice way to un-wind. Especially after the fire."

"O-kay. But you do know they don't serve green juice, right?" Midnight said in a cautious voice, well aware of her mom's thoughts on refined sugar. Then she widened her eyes. "Is this for market research?"

"Of course not," her mom said before suddenly coughing. "I mean yes. That's right. Market research.

After all, my own café's opening in less than a month. Besides, I thought it'd be fun. Unless you have something else planned?"

You mean like looking for the missing planodiume?

Like stopping people from getting hurt?

Like waiting for Peter Gallagher to call back?

"No." Midnight forced herself to stop thinking about her job. Thankfully, over the last nine months she'd gotten pretty good at compartmentalizing her life.

Of course it had become easier now that Tabitha and Logan were in on her secret. Because hiding it from her friends had led to a whole lot of misunderstandings. She'd also told her seventeen-year-old sister about her special abilities, after they'd rescued her from her crazy ex-boyfriend who'd tried to kill them all using planodiume.

Midnight had even been tempted to tell her mom about her ghost-hunting job, but Taylor had talked her out of it. And she'd been right.

If their mom knew Midnight faced mortal danger on a daily basis, she'd probably ground her for the next hundred years, and by default, she'd probably ground Taylor too.

The whole situation wasn't ideal, but at least her spreadsheets had helped. A separate cell for every problem.

She got out of the car to follow her mom and Phil into Cookies and Cakes. It would be weird to be here with them, but she wasn't the kind of girl to look a gift horse in the mouth. Especially when that gift horse was chocolate-flavored.

"You probably won't need your backpack." Her mom eyed the bulging bag Midnight had hooked over her shoulder.

She gulped and tightened her grip on the purple straps.

In it was one of the smaller carbonic resonators she used to release spectral energy, as well as her Ping. It was one thing to compartmentalize her life, but it was another thing to walk around without any protection. Especially in light of what had just happened at the circus.

"Actually, it's probably better to take it in with her," Phil said in his mild voice as he put an arm around her mom's slim shoulder. "There've been a few break-ins recently. I've had three damaged cars come into the garage in the past week. Better safe than sorry."

"I had no idea. I guess we all need to be careful these

days," her mom said as they walked into the brightly lit café.

A cute pale-pink sign hung in the window, and the decor was white and modern with pale wooden chairs and tables. The scent of vanilla and sugar hung in the air. Midnight's mouth watered.

A long cabinet ran along the counter with a seemingly never-ending selection of cakes and cookies, all the colors of the rainbow. She searched out her favorite double fudge with vanilla frosting and let out a happy sigh. Still three slices left.

"So, Midnight, what will it be?" Phil's gaze drifted from the pecan pie over to a plate of red velvet cupcakes. Midnight pointed out her cake while Phil settled on the pie. Her mom ordered a pot of herbal tea, and they headed to a table.

"You might as well tell me what's going on," Midnight said once they were settled.

"Honey, there's nothing going on," her mom said a little too quickly as she tapped the table with her fingers, her silver rings gleaming. "I've just been so busy setting up the café and organizing our very first summer solstice party that I didn't want you to feel neglected. Think of this as quality time together."

"Um, thanks," Midnight said.

"Don't be silly." Her mom pushed back one of her blond curls and let out a soft sigh. "Though, as it happens, there *is* something we wanted to discuss with—"

"Phil! Maggie! Oh, and look, it's Midnight." A voice roared from across the café as a tall man with a red beard and long red hair hanging down his back in a braid walked toward them. Jerry Van Meek was part of Phil's Viking reenactment society. He was closely followed by several other off-duty Vikings. Midnight recognized them from her mom's wedding, though now, as they clambered around the table, she realized just how noisy they were.

"This is a pleasant surprise," one of them boomed. "We'd planned to go to the circus, but it was canceled so we thought we'd stop by here. Mind if we join you?"

Her mom exchanged a small glance with Phil, so miniscule that Midnight doubted anyone else had seen it. Then Phil nodded and held out his hands.

"The more, the merrier," he said just as the server appeared with the cake, pie, and drinks.

Midnight let out a relieved sigh. Whatever her mom wanted to discuss must've been serious considering she was using cake for bribery, but right now Midnight had enough to deal with.

So while the rest of the group talked about the upcoming solstice feast, she busied herself with the important task of eating her cake and checking her text messages. There was one from Tabitha.

Any news from Peter?

Midnight's mom—who didn't approve of texting at the table—was having an intense conversation about the benefits of using flaxseeds instead of eggs for baking. Midnight lowered her phone into her lap.

No. I'm at C&C with my mom and Phil.

You're eating cake while we're in the middle of a crisis? Tabitha's reply boomeranged back.

Yup. Midnight sent a line of cake emoticons.

Now I'm hungry too. LMK when you hear something.

Will do. Midnight hit Send just as her mom glanced over. She quickly raised her hands onto the table and allowed herself to be dragged into a heated debate about whether the original Vikings ate potatoes.

By the time they were ready to leave, Midnight was half-asleep and her mom didn't seem eager to start discussing whatever she'd wanted to discuss. Which was a good thing. All Midnight wanted was to figure out her next move.

Chapter Three

"It's *what*?" Midnight said the following morning as she sat on the end of her bed with her phone.

"Spectral transference," Peter Gallagher repeated in his clipped English accent. Thanks to his job, he was always traveling and often couldn't call back right away. At least this time he hadn't woken her up in the middle of the night.

Not that she'd slept well.

She'd tossed and turned, dreaming of the strange golden swirls and the flames of the mysterious fire. The good news was Tabitha's dad said the clown was going to be okay. He was in the hospital with second-degree burns and a broken leg, but that was nothing he wouldn't recover from.

The bad news was Peter Gallagher sounded worried. If it had been a video call, Midnight was certain his jaw would be tight and lines would be running down the sides of his mouth.

"Spectral transference? Why haven't I heard of it before?" After her last case, her security clearance level had increased, which meant she had access to a lot more information in the Agency of Spectral Protection's files. But nowhere had she seen any mention of spectral transference.

"Because it's not common. Last year we only had five instances." Peter sounded tired. "It's what happens when spectral energy is drawn out of a living person."

Midnight's jaw dropped.

"How's that even possible?" she finally whispered. "I thought spectral energy only happened *after* someone had died."

"It's a bit more complicated. The particles exist in our bodies but don't get released until after the heart stops.

However, several weapons have been designed to extract it early. In essence, it's like they're stealing time from people."

"That's what happened to the clown? Some of his life was stolen?"

There was silence from the other end of the line before Peter finally coughed. "I'm afraid so. We've had several cases where it was just a small amount. But the more that's taken, the sicker a person gets. They prematurely age, and their organs start to shut down. If too much is stolen, then they will—"

The words hung in the air, and Midnight swallowed. He didn't have to say it out loud because she knew what he meant. *Die.*

"So, this is serious?"

"Very." His voice was grim. "The only way the victims can have their stolen energy returned is if you can release it from whatever it's trapped in. We need to solve it soon, before the circus leaves town."

Midnight stared at her spreadsheet. Her date with Logan at the swimming pool on Wednesday was blocked out in yellow. Her chances to kiss Logan were taking up a lot of time in her schedule. As much as she wanted the kiss to happen, she had to make sure no one else was hurt by spectral transference.

"I'll do everything I can," she promised, reluctantly deleting all the cells that had been colored pale yellow.

"Thank you." The relief was evident in his voice. "And the reason your sonic detector didn't go off is because it only measures spectral energy that's trapped in an inanimate object. It can't pick it up when it's being sent straight from a living person. Which means you won't have an advanced warning system. You're going into this blind."

Midnight touched her glasses. They were what allowed her to see spectral energy, and without them she was as clueless as everyone else. Well, not quite. She could still *feel* it, but without being able to see it, the energy transference would be almost impossible to stop.

Still, Peter didn't mean she'd literally be blind; just that she couldn't rely on technology like she usually did.

"At least I won't be alone." Midnight pressed her lips together, grateful she had friends to watch her back.

"I wasn't sure about bringing civilians to the Agency, but Tabitha and Logan have certainly proven their worth. I suggest you talk to the clown. See what he can remember. Also, if you can get close enough, your sonic detector will indicate how much energy was stolen from him. You need to set it to Level D."

"What does the D stand for?" Midnight said, not sure she really wanted to know the answer. *Death?*

"Deficiency. It's measured in median units known as SEDs," Peter replied crisply as she scrambled to retrieve her Ping and scrolled through the screen prompts until she found the correct level. "To maintain full health, a person needs one hundred percent spectral energy. The more that's taken, the more the person's health will be affected."

"How much is too much?" Midnight frowned. Math wasn't her best subject, and she hadn't planned to do much of it over the summer break.

"Our data indicates that if less than ten percent SED is detected, a person might not even notice the difference. At twenty percent, they might feel like they've got the flu and can typically expect to lose a year of their natural life. However, the more SED that's been removed, the faster the degeneration occurs. The tipping point is fifty percent, and by eighty percent, heart failure will set in."

"That's not good." Midnight swallowed.

"Agreed. If you can get a reading from the victim, it will help us know what we're up against."

Panic flooded her mind. How was she going to convince a sick clown to talk to some middle-school kids?

She shook it away. She had her friends. They'd figure it out together.

"I'll let you know how we do," she said. "What happens if I see spectral transference happening again? Will my weapons work on it?"

"I'll need to consult the research department. Hold on." He returned several minutes later. "We really don't know. For now, take one of your carbonic resonators, and be careful. I don't have to remind you how dangerous this might be."

"I'll be careful," she promised just as a crashing noise came from downstairs in the kitchen.

"*Noooooo*," her mom wailed. This was followed by a sharp howl, as something pounded up the stairs, sharp claws dragging along the wooden floorboards.

"Everything okay?" Peter asked as Midnight jumped to her feet.

"I don't know, but I'm about to find out." She said a quick goodbye and reached for CARA, her weapon of choice. The device was a tangle of brass and copper tubes that looked like a trumpet with a wooden handle and a glass canister running along the top. Her fingers tightened around the handle. Her Ping hadn't gone off, and there was no buzzing noise in her ears, but if Peter Gallagher was right, she could no longer trust the Ping to help her out.

The sound retreated, as if the creature was heading back the way it had come. Back to her mother. Midnight pushed open the door and raced downstairs.

"Mom. What's going on? Are you okay?" She sprinted along the hallway just as a ball of black-and-white fur hurtled toward her.

Midnight came to a screeching halt.

A puppy?

She quickly thrust CARA behind her back as her mom appeared in the doorway. Her curly hair was in disarray, and her mouth was set in a frustrated line that Midnight knew only too well.

"What's all the noise?" Taylor emerged from the living

room, arms folded. She had long, blond hair that made her look like a model.

Her sister's gaze narrowed as she noticed the weapon behind Midnight's back.

Without speaking, Taylor joined her, so close that their shoulders touched, in an effort to conceal it. They waited until their mom picked up the wriggling puppy before they shuffled to the wall and Midnight deposited CARA behind the laundry basket sitting on the floor.

Thankfully, their mom was too distracted with the puppy to notice.

Midnight wanted to wipe her brow. That was way too close.

"Okay, I'll bite," Taylor said. "Mom, why's there a puppy in the house?"

"Isn't she cute? This is Rita. She's a six-month-old border collie. She belongs to Jessie from down the road. Her brother just had a heart attack, and she's flying to California to be with him. Thankfully, she remembered that Midnight's been doing a lot of babysitting lately." Their mom walked back into the kitchen.

"Wait. *What?* I can't babysit a puppy." Midnight's

throat tightened. She wasn't really a sitter. It was just the cover she used for her job at ASP.

She followed her mom into the kitchen, and her eyes grew wide.

The place was a mess. On the floor were a broken crystal vase and a roll of toilet paper that had been shredded to pieces, as well as a pair of slippers covered in slobber.

"Why not?" her mom asked. "You're off school for the entire summer, and it's a nice way for you to earn some extra money. I thought you'd be thrilled."

"This place is hardly puppy-proof." Taylor arched an eyebrow and glanced around at the numerous pieces of Viking paraphernalia that dotted the kitchen. An ax leaned against the wall, while several shields were flat on the table where Phil had been oiling them. Not to mention the heavy chain mail draped over a chair.

"I'm sure it won't take us long to get everything sorted out," her mom replied.

"But I can't dog sit." Midnight tried to stop the rising panic in her stomach. Not that she didn't like puppies. After all, they were cute and furry. Particularly this one, who had a patch of black over one eye and a patch of white over the other. But she had to go to the hospital to investigate a spectral transference incident, and she could hardly do that with a puppy tucked under her arm. Nor could she tell her mom. "The thing is—"

"I'll dog sit," Taylor cut in, and their mom blinked in surprise.

In the past Taylor hadn't always been the most helpful family member. But now that she knew what Midnight's job was, and how dangerous trapped spectral energy could be, she seemed happier to help cover for her. Problem was, their mom didn't know that.

"I thought you and Donna were camping this week," their mom said, confused. "You've been talking about it for the last four months."

"I've changed my mind. I think it might rain." Taylor turned her back to the summery blue sky outside the window. Their mom looked like she wanted to say more, but before she could, Rita opened an eye and began to wriggle again.

"Okay, but Midnight, I still expect you to help your sister." Their mom handed the small ball of black-and-white fur to Taylor, who wrinkled her nose in distaste as the puppy immediately clawed at her new T-shirt.

Old Taylor would've freaked out. Taylor 2.0 seemed to be taking it all in stride.

"Thanks." Midnight whispered as their mom turned her attention to the broken vase on the floor. "I owe you, big-time."

"It's fine." Taylor awkwardly tried to hold the little creature. Then, without another word, she headed for the stairs and took the puppy up to her bedroom.

"I can see our new houseguest has been busy." Phil appeared in the doorway with a steel helmet on his head, a handmade leather tunic over his chest, and a box of doughnuts in his hand. He paused to kiss Midnight's mom before looking around the wrecked kitchen. "And speaking of Rita, where is she?"

"Taylor's taken her up to her room," Midnight's mom said.

"*Taylor's* looking after her?" Phil's jaw dropped as he put an arm around his wife's shoulder. "I guess you were right."

"Right about what?" Midnight frowned. "What's going on?"

Her mom sighed. "I wanted to talk to you about it last night. That's why we stopped for cake."

"You wanted to talk about Taylor?" Midnight said in surprise.

Her mom nodded. "She's been acting strangely ever since she broke up with Dylan. Has she said anything to you?"

You mean about her boyfriend being evil?

That he used the souls of the dead to steal things?

And that he tried to hurt her?

"Er, no." Midnight quickly shook her head. Which was kind of true. They might be closer than they'd once been, but it wasn't like they talked about boyfriends. It also proved there was no such thing as free cake. "I'm sure she's fine."

"Midnight. Your sister just offered to babysit a puppy." Her mom quirked an eyebrow and retrieved the broom while Phil stacked up his Viking weapons. Midnight busied herself with the shredded toilet paper to avoid her mom's supersonic gaze. "This is the girl who didn't let me vacuum her room in case I touched her things."

"W-well, perhaps she's trying to change?" Midnight put the mounds of paper into the trash can and tried to ignore the crashing sound coming from upstairs.

She knew the whole reason Taylor was acting differently was because she'd almost been killed by spectral energy. Midnight swallowed down her guilt. If she'd warned her sister earlier about what her boyfriend had been up to, the situation might have been avoided.

She couldn't afford to make the same mistakes again. Until she'd caught whoever was stealing spectral energy and turning it into planodiume, everything else—even her date with Logan—had to be taken off her spreadsheet.

"And what's more, I bumped into Donna's mom two days ago," her mom said. "She was asking if Taylor was okay because she hadn't been around there in weeks."

Midnight didn't know what to say to that, but she was saved from answering by the appearance of Tabitha in the kitchen doorway. She was wearing black jeans, black Doc Martens, and a short-sleeved black T-shirt, in concession to the morning warmth.

"Sorry, I'm late. My mom got stuck in traffic." Her friend peered at the mess. "What happened here?"

"It's a long story," Midnight said before her mom could start explaining.

Right now she had another long story to share with Tabitha. About something a lot more dangerous than a mischievous puppy.

CHAPTER FOUR

"You're telling me that we don't even know if our weapons will work?" Tabitha said as they stood in front of Berry Centennial Hospital two hours later. Logan had been roped into babysitting Bella, so he hadn't been able to come.

"Pretty much." Midnight nodded. "There haven't been enough reported cases for ASP to test any weapons against spectral transference. We're the guinea pigs."

"That's not comforting." Tabitha shivered underneath her black T-shirt as they walked up the path.

Midnight hoped they'd be able to speak to the clown

and see what he remembered about his accident. Of course he wouldn't know it was spectral energy, but there might have been something he'd seen or heard. Anything that could help give them a clue to who was behind it.

The hospital was an old Victorian building with redbrick walls and small windows, all surrounded by swaying oak trees. In winter it was eerie and sinister, but with the summer sun and an explosion of color in the flower beds, the place looked almost inviting.

The metallic waft of antiseptic greeted them as they walked up to the reception desk in the lobby.

Thanks to Tabitha's father, they already knew the clown's name: Joseph Alexander. He'd been with the circus for ten years as it traveled around the United States, and this was the first time he'd ever been injured. The one thing they didn't know was his room number.

"Should we go over our cover story one more time?" Midnight kept her voice low.

"Okay." Tabitha composed her face into a suitably serious expression. "While most kids prefer to fritter away their summer break at the pool, swimming and relaxing, we want to volunteer to spend time with people who don't have relatives to keep them company. *With particular interest in clowns.*"

"Perfect," Midnight said. "But I don't think we need the clown bit at the end."

"Don't worry. I won't mess up," Tabitha promised as they reached the reception desk.

"Can I help you girls?" A bald man at the desk looked up from the crossword he was working on.

"Yes, please. We're looking for Joseph Alexander," Tabitha said. "You see, while most kids—"

"Room twenty-two, in the blue wing," the guy said before returning his attention to the puzzle. Tabitha blinked, and Midnight quickly dragged her away before her friend could say anything else.

"Rude much?" Tabitha protested. "He didn't even let me finish telling him why we wanted to visit. How am I meant to get better at cover stories if no one will let me practice?"

"Don't you think it's better that we didn't need the cover story?" Midnight suggested. "Especially since it's not true."

"He didn't know that." Tabitha scowled. "This place has lousy security."

"Thank goodness," Midnight said as they followed the blue arrow down the wide corridor. Their shoes squeaked on the linoleum floors as they walked past several waiting rooms filled with tired-looking people. They increased their pace. Even though Tabitha loved cemeteries, and Midnight had fought danger on a regular basis, both of them were creeped out by hospitals.

"Finally." Tabitha blew out a column of air as they reached room twenty-two. The door was open, and they peered inside. The man in the bed had streaky blond hair. His arm was wrapped in a white bandage, and his leg was in a cast.

"If you're here to give me any more needles, you can think again. I'm not a pincushion," he snapped before looking up. "Oh, you're just kids."

"Sorry to interrupt you," Midnight said, holding her hands up to show she wasn't armed with needles. For some reason, she'd expected off-duty clowns to be friendly. A bit like Santa Claus. "Are you Joseph Alexander?"

"Who's asking?" The grumpy clown started to fold his arm before wincing. He'd obviously forgotten about the burns he'd received.

"I'm Tabitha, and this is my friend Midnight. My dad rescued you last night," she said, and some of the hostility in his face softened.

"Oh. Come in." He nodded for them to enter and leaned back into the pillows, as if the conversation had taken it out of him. "John swung by earlier to see how I was doing. He's a good guy."

"We wanted to ask you a few questions about last night's accident," Midnight said.

"Why? What's it got to do with a couple of kids?" He raised a thin eyebrow.

She bit down on her lip. It would be so much easier if they could just tell him the truth about what had happened. That way he'd be more likely to help them.

Or, he'd think we were crazy.

"I know it's summer break, but Midnight and I are working on our next English paper. All the kids will go back to school, writing about their lame visits to the beach." Tabitha took over, moving to the second part of their cover story. "But we want to do our story on your accident, so we figured we'd get some insider information. It'll look great on our college applications."

Midnight was impressed. She could hardly think about eighth grade, let alone college, but Tabitha's speech seemed to do the trick and Joseph let out a long sigh.

"Fine. Ask away."

"What do you remember about last night?" Midnight asked.

"Not much. I did my normal show. I'm an Auguste clown, not to be mistaken with a whiteface clown. Not that people care. They think clowning's all about laughing and smiling. But I'm old school. That means once I'm in character, I stay in character."

"There's a difference?" Tabitha raised an eyebrow.

"Yes, there's a difference." Joseph growled. "The makeup for a start. I'd *never* use white powder. Plus, my outfits are always exaggerated. With the big collars, huge shirts, and wide pants, I look almost double the size. I tell you, it's an art form."

"Oh." Tabitha nodded, looking like she was sorry she'd asked. "So, what happened next?"

"There I was, being clumsy when I did my *blow-off*—that's what we call a set piece, in the business. It went down fine. The crowd ate it up. And then...I started to feel dizzy, and everything went black. Next thing, I'm waking up in an ambulance with burns on my arm and a broken leg."

"You don't remember seeing anything?" Midnight persisted.

"Nope." Joseph shook his head. "But I'll tell you this for free… It wasn't an accident."

"What makes you say that?" Tabitha looked up from her notepad.

"Because there's no way I would've dropped those flames. I've practiced that move thousands of times before. It's like breathing. If you ask me, someone tampered with the baton."

"Any idea who?" Midnight leaned forward.

He shrugged. "Any number of people. Clowning's a blood sport. There's always some smart aleck coming up through the ranks, trying to get your spot. And then there's the public. These days everyone hates us. I blame that Stephen King book."

Tabitha tilted her head, and a ghost of a smile tugged at her mouth. "Curious. And what are your thoughts on aliens? Real or fake?"

"Please, we all know Roswell's real. The government's been hiding alien abductions for years…" He started to prattle.

Midnight blinked. Why was Tabitha asking such a random question? Then she noticed that Tabitha was waving her Ping behind her back, enthusiastically nodding as the clown ranted about Area 51.

Oh. *That* was why she'd let him go on a tangent.

Midnight casually slipped her own device out and activated it before edging her way closer to the bed.

"…and do you have *any* idea why aliens only abduct farmers? It's because of the high levels of methane," Joseph was saying. Midnight angled herself to hide the device, which was hovering close to his broken leg.

Ping. Ping. Ping.

She coughed to cover the noise as Joseph narrowed his eyes.

"What was that?" he demanded as she quickly slipped it back into her pocket.

"What was *what*?" She gave him her best vacuous gaze. It was the same one her sister used to get out of washing the dishes.

Just then a nurse pushed in a cart with a needle gleaming brightly on the tray.

"I'm sorry. Visiting hours are over."

"Oh." Midnight nodded before turning to Joseph. The rant had brought the color back to his face. "Thanks for helping. I hope you feel better soon."

"Doubtful." His mouth flattened into a stubborn line. "Do you have any idea how many people come to these places fit and healthy and then get sick once they arrive?"

"Excuse me?" the nurse protested. "I'll have you know that certainly doesn't happen on my watch."

"Yeah, yeah," the clown muttered. "Just give me the stupid needle. Oh, and tell that annoying candy striper not to bother bringing me any books. I hate reading."

"She's only trying to help you," the nurse said in a gentle voice before turning to the girls and nodding for them to leave. They were just about to step through the door, when Tabitha stopped and spun around.

"Just one more question about your accident," she said. "Do you remember hearing some kind of hissing?"

"A hiss?" His voice dropped to a whisper. "You saw it too?"

"*Saw* it?" Midnight looked up. She'd heard the noise, but all she'd seen was spectral energy. Had she missed something? "What did you see?"

"It looked like a golden snake. It was coiled up, ready to strike."

"Why didn't you tell us before?" Tabitha asked as she scribbled down notes.

"Because I didn't want anyone to think I was crazy." His Adam's apple bobbed in his throat.

"Why's that so crazy? It's a circus. Wouldn't a snake belong to one of the acts?" Midnight asked.

Joseph shook his head. "We're an animal-free circus. There are no snakes."

Midnight's mouth fell open, but before she could ask any more questions, the nurse made a coughing noise and glanced at the door. They waited until they got outside before looking at each other.

"Okay, next time Logan's going to do the undercover work," Tabitha said with a shudder. "People are just too difficult. Still, at least we know a few things. Well, one. That there might've been a golden snake."

"A golden snake that only *he* saw." Midnight rubbed

her brow, before suddenly remembering the Ping. She dragged it from her pocket. "And, we got a reading. That was a brilliant diversion."

"I thought so," Tabitha agreed as they both studied the device's screen.

SED: 0.05%

Life-Span Depletion: 5 hours.

"So, he's lost five hours of his natural life." Some of the panic left Midnight's chest. In the grand scheme of things, five hours wasn't so bad. It wasn't great, of course, but if they could find the person responsible, hopefully nothing worse would happen.

The same bald guy was at the reception desk, talking to a woman with black hair tied into a neat bun at the base of her neck and wearing denim jeans and long, black boots. It was Zelda the Great.

"She must be friends with Joseph," Midnight said as Zelda headed in the direction they'd just come from. If she'd recognized them as the girls who had stood outside her tent the previous day, she didn't let on.

"Yeah, though if she's such a good fortune-teller, why didn't she warn him what was going to happen?" Tabitha muttered as they left the hospital and headed to the town library to do more research. Hopefully, they'd find something that would actually give them a clue.

CHAPTER FIVE

"I could've come to your place." Logan jogged over to the park bench, leaving a trail of footprints in the glistening dew that still covered the grass. His eyes were bright, and he was wearing one of his many Sherlock Holmes T-shirts. This one said *Baker Street or Bust.*

Midnight had called him yesterday to break their date and explain why she had to focus on the case. Work had to come first. People's lives might depend on it. He'd been great, but part of her still wished they could've gone ahead with their trip to the swimming pool.

"Trust me, you don't want to go there. There's a puppy

that thinks she's descended from Attila the Hun. I'm talking wrecking machine. I was there ten minutes, and look what she did to my boot." Tabitha thrust out the studded black ankle boot that she'd spent six months' allowance on.

She was more of a cat person.

"You got a puppy?" Logan raised an eyebrow. "Bella will be so jealous."

"Not exactly." Midnight shook her head. "Our neighbor had to go away unexpectedly, and my mom thought since I did so much babysitting I'd be okay to do some dog sitting."

Logan immediately seemed to grasp the irony of the situation.

"Ouch. Trapped by your own lie." He pushed his sneaker against the gravel, creating a scraping noise as worry marred his features. "So, is this spectral transference thing really as bad as it sounds?"

"Worse." Tabitha opened the folder of documents she'd printed. "These are from the ASP's archives. Peter wasn't exaggerating about how little they know. I did some online research, but I couldn't find much."

"I still can't believe you saw the clown's eyes change color." Logan let out a wistful sigh.

"Trust me, it was something I could've done without." Midnight shuddered. It wasn't the first time she'd seen someone's physical appearance change because of planodiume. But in those cases, it was because the person had been misusing it, and their eyes had turned black. This had been different. She just wasn't sure how.

"Tell me everything Joseph said." Logan quickly changed the topic, as if realizing how uncomfortable she felt. She gave him a grateful smile. Tabitha ignored them both and frowned some more.

"He's a conspiracy nut who's convinced everyone's out to get him. The only thing he told us was he saw a golden snake."

Logan frowned. "In an animal-free circus? No wonder it stood out. I can't think of any snakes that are golden in color, but there are plenty of yellow ones."

"You don't think it's a figment of his imagination?" Tabitha blanched. "Because I don't do snakes."

"They're not my favorite thing either, but at this stage we have to be open," Logan said as they climbed on the bus. "We might as well start looking for snakes."

As far as plans went, it wasn't great. But the idea

of someone running around Berry stealing spectral energy—and therefore life—from people was even worse.

* * *

"Of course I remember you," Carlo the ringmaster said an hour later. There were dark lines under his hooded eyes, but his smile was still bright. "You're John Wilson's daughter, Tabitha. And you're Midnight. I remember thinking what a great stage name that would make."

Midnight gritted her teeth. At least he hadn't made a joke about it, which was what usually happened. *Creepy Hour. Tick Tock. Clock Face.*

"That's right," Tabitha quickly said, as if sensing Midnight's mood. "This is our friend, Logan."

"Nice to meet you," Logan said in a polite voice. "Up until the accident, the first show was amazing."

"Thank you." Carlo ushered them under the wide awning that stretched out along his Winnebago. A folding table and chairs had been set up, and there were stacks of paperwork, held down by a shoe to keep them from blowing away. "Sorry about the mess. Running a circus is chaotic at the best of times…and…let's just say this *hasn't* been the best of times."

"Because of the accident?" Midnight asked.

"Yes. I've been up half the night dealing with police reports and insurance claims as well as media inquiries. Makes me wish Eduardo was still here to give me a helping hand." He rubbed his chin and yawned. "Sorry. You probably don't want to hear about my problems. How can I help you kids?"

"A-actually, it's about the accident. We were wondering how Joseph's doing," Midnight said, crossing her fingers. Her nose didn't seem to grow from telling the lie.

Carlo sucked in a dramatic breath as long, dark hair fell around his face. "He'll be out by the end of the week, but it's such a tragedy."

"Has anything like this happened before?" Tabitha asked.

An odd look crossed Carlo's face, and it took a moment for him to answer.

"We've never had a single accident until now." Carlo's dark eyes seemed blank, as if they couldn't quite focus. Then he blinked a few times and gave the friends another Hollywood smile. "It's something we've always prided ourselves on. Still, as they say, 'the show must go on.'"

"Speaking of the show, who'll take Joseph's place?" Logan asked. Midnight and Tabitha both gave him an approving nod. He was trying to find out if anyone had a motive to injure Joseph.

Carlo didn't seem perturbed by the question. "We wouldn't dream of bringing in another clown."

"I see." Logan studied his notepad. "Did he have many friends here?"

"Friends?" Carlo opened his arms expansively toward the many performers who were walking past the awning. "Here at the Cirque Fantastic, we aren't just friends, we're family. What affects one affects all."

"I understand." Logan's brows creased together, but before he could say anything else, Carlo glanced at his watch.

"And now I must prepare for our matinee performance."

"Of course. Though, out of curiosity, does anyone at the circus have a pet snake?" Tabitha asked.

"A snake?" He blinked in genuine surprise. "Definitely not."

"Thanks," Midnight said, and they headed back out into the crowd.

Even though word of the fire had spread, it hadn't stopped people from turning up. Carnival music blasted from speakers, and in the distance they could hear high-pitched screams from the many rides that swooped and swirled through the air.

"Logan, did you get any clues?" Midnight asked in a hopeful voice.

"Sorry." He shook his head. "If he's hiding something, he's doing a really good job of it. Though there were a lot of papers on the table. We could look through them while he's performing in the big top."

"It's too risky. But there's more than one way to snoop." Tabitha swung her backpack off her shoulder and patted it. Inside was her MacBook. "I'll start digging up information on Carlo, and you guys can see what you can find out about snakes and accidents."

Midnight nodded. "We'll meet up in an hour."

"Sounds great." Tabitha's eyes glittered with determination before she turned and walked to the wooded area behind the House of Mirrors.

"Carlo will have to be a great magician to hide anything from her." Midnight giggled.

"Agreed." Logan gave her a half smile as he toed the ground with his sneaker. When he looked up, his cheeks were flushed. "I think we should go to the amusement tents. We can play a few games and ask some questions."

Midnight, who hadn't been sure where to start, nodded. "That sounds great."

"Though I warn you, when it comes to the Laughing Clowns, I'm an expert." His voice was serious, but a cute smile tugged at his mouth.

"Is that a challenge?"

"Definitely."

They wove their way through the crowds toward the carnival games, their shoulders almost rubbing so they didn't get separated. They reached a green-striped tent where seven open-mouthed clown heads moved slowly back and forth, blank eyes looking out into the distance.

"Step right up. Two dollars will buy you five balls." The woman working the stand had salt-and-pepper hair and layers of jewelry around her neck. "Test your skills, and win one of our glorious prizes."

Along the back wall was an explosion of ugly stuffed

animals, much like the one Logan had won for Bella. Midnight stifled a giggle.

"Do you have any snakes?" she asked.

"No. This year everyone wants bears and dinosaurs," the woman said.

"I'll take ten balls." Logan handed over some money.

"Let's see how you do." The woman passed him two red cups, each filled with five balls. In turn, he gave one cup to Midnight.

"So, have you been busy today?" He fed his first ball into the clown's mouth.

"Meh." The old woman gave an indifferent shrug. "Just average. Being shut down yesterday didn't help."

"I can imagine." He took out a second ball and studied it before peering at her through his dark lashes. "I was actually in the audience on the first day. It was so freaky. Anything like that ever happened before?"

Her gaze suddenly went blank. "There's never any accidents," she said, her voice almost robotic. A second later, her blank look was gone and she turned to a couple of young kids walking toward the stall. "Step right up, step right up…"

Midnight lowered her voice. "Carlo said the same thing. That there are never any accidents. What if the fire was just a coincidence?"

"It's a possibility," Logan agreed as she put the next ball in the clown's mouth, aiming for the same target as the last one. But just as she released the ball, he gave her a soft nudge and it went awry.

"Hey. You did that on purpose."

"I told you, I take my Laughing Clowns seriously." He dropped another ball in. Midnight nudged him back, and he let out a groan.

"You're not the only one," she said, and the pair of them burst out laughing. The old woman gave them a dark glare as they handed back their cups.

They spent the next half hour going from tent to tent, buying tickets, attempting to win ugly stuffed animals, buying food and large sticks of cotton candy, all while asking the people who ran the games about the accident. And each answer was the same, delivered with a blank-eyed but resolute reply.

There'd *never* been any accidents at Cirque Fantastic.

"Is it wrong that I had fun?" Midnight finished her soda,

her jaw aching from all the smiling. It turned out Logan didn't just like winning at the Laughing Clowns. Everything he did was with a mock seriousness that made her giggle.

"Me too," he said as they walked away from the stall toward the rides. Screams rang out as the giant mechanical arms swung people around in the air, swooshing as they went past. "Then again, I always have fun when we hang out."

He did?

"I'm sorry we couldn't go to the swimming pool today," she said.

Logan stopped walking, his gaze catching hers. A nervous smile hovered on his lips, and she caught her breath. *Is he going to kiss me right here? Right now?*

"It's okay," he said before leaning closer. "Do you know you have chocolate on your chin?"

"Oh." She didn't move as he lightly touched her face with his finger.

Noise exploded in her ears. A thousand bees buzzing. *Noooooo.*

Of all the times for spectral energy to turn up, it had to be now?

Her skin prickled as she reluctantly looked around to discover a delicate tendril of pink fog hovering several feet away from her.

Eliza Irongate! Or, what was left of her.

Eliza had been born in 1883 and died in 1895. Murdered by Miss Appleby, the first person to know of Midnight's special abilities. Midnight had worked with Miss Appleby until she realized the old woman had been misusing spectral energy to stay alive for more than a century. Midnight had no choice but to destroy Miss Appleby and release all the trapped spectral energy so it could go to the Afterglow, and she thought she'd never see the spirit of the twelve-year-old girl again. But then Eliza had returned to stop Taylor's ex-boyfriend from killing them. Which meant if she was here now, it was for one reason only.

To help.

"Everything okay?" The soft look in Logan's eyes had been replaced by confusion. Midnight didn't blame him. In the past, she'd often been forced to cut short their conversations because of spectral energy. And while it should've made her feel better that at least she could tell him *why* she had to go, it didn't.

Because the truth was that right now she'd rather be a normal girl, just hanging out with Logan. Unfortunately, she wasn't.

"It's Eliza. I think she's trying to show me something," Midnight said as the pink fog turned and snaked through the crowded carnival.

"Let's go see what it is," Logan replied.

"Thanks." Having a friend by her side certainly made following a ghostly spirit less daunting.

The buzzing in her ears increased, but the icy panic that often accompanied planodiume was gone. With Eliza, she was safe.

The soft, pink tendril sped past rows of tents, moving faster and faster. Midnight panted as Eliza twisted her way past several more rides and campers.

"Hey, watch it," someone protested.

"Sorry," she called out, not slowing down.

She was jogging now, her breath coming in short bursts as Eliza disappeared. Midnight came to a halt before seeing the shimmer of pink hovering just above a small tent. It was faded purple, like a squashed grape.

There was no mistaking what Eliza was trying to tell her.

Go inside.

Logan caught up with her. "Should I come with you?" His eyes filled with concern. Midnight shook her head.

"We've got no idea what's in there. I'll go in, and you can call Tabitha."

Logan opened his mouth as if he wanted to protest. Then he gave her a quick nod. "Okay. But be careful."

"I will," she said and then took a deep breath as Eliza began to flicker. Her pale colors became infused with dark streaks of gray, angry like a bruise.

Whatever Eliza was trying to show her was obviously urgent. Midnight stepped forward into the tent.

Chapter Six

Despite the blazing sun, the tent was filled with inky darkness. Midnight was tempted to use her phone as a flashlight, but she had no idea what was waiting for her. Eliza's soft, rosy hues offered enough light for Midnight to move forward into a long corridor. From the outside, the tent hadn't been much bigger than a phone booth, yet inside, the end of it was nowhere in sight. She shivered.

The floor was covered with layers of carpet that let her move silently forward while the walls pulsed and swayed as she passed them. She tightened her grip on her backpack as Eliza continued forward into a large room.

Midnight came to an abrupt halt.

The enormous space was illuminated by a glittering chandelier that was sending prisms of light bouncing out, while the walls were covered with huge circus posters. They were old and faded, like the tent's exterior.

One was a lion tamer, and another was a muscular man sitting on top of a cannon. A third had a woman standing on top of an elephant, and the final one was a picture of the same old-fashioned ringmaster who'd been on the circus posters plastered all over town.

Carlo's long-dead relative, Eduardo De Rossi.

The family resemblance was strong, but Eduardo had glossier hair and a mesmerizing smile that glowed against the dull light. A tall top hat was perched on his head at a rakish angle, and his dark eyes seemed to drill into her through the paper.

It's just a poster.

Eliza darted in front of her vision as if to break the thrall.

Midnight turned away. Everywhere she looked was circus memorabilia, almost like in a museum.

A single ornate golden carousel horse from one of the carnival rides was propped up against a huge barrel, while next to it was a small cage on wheels, its bars still gleaming so brightly she had to shield her eyes.

There were more cages farther around. Bigger, and all looking as if animals had once been inside them. To the left was an old hot-dog cart, as well as a pile of glittering costumes and a rack of swords—their blades deadly sharp.

Behind them were shelves and shelves of smaller items. Reels of unused tickets, an old-fashioned megaphone, a coiled whip. Several mirrors that warped her reflection were propped against a wall, and there was a dressing table full of wigs and tubes of face paint.

And in the center of the room was a coffin-shaped box perched on a table covered with a tasseled purple cloth.

The pink fog disappeared under the table with the same panicked urgency it had used to get Midnight into the tent. She gulped. The purple tassels trailed along the floor, and the idea of poking her hand under there didn't fill her with joy.

Eliza's color darkened from pale pink to a dull red, and Midnight reluctantly lifted the cloth. There was nothing there. Then she narrowed her eyes. Almost camouflaged against the rug was a balled-up piece of paper.

Midnight stretched out for it as the lights in the room darkened and a soft wind swirled around her ankles.

Something was happening.

Her fingers tightened on the paper, and she scrambled away from the table as the cloth fluttered in the growing breeze and the silhouette of a body floated just above it.

Midnight stifled a scream.

The silhouette was dark, but as the gusts of cold air quickened, patches of the figure turned to gold in the flickering light, making it look like an unfinished three-dimensional jigsaw puzzle.

More golden pieces appeared until she could see the faint shape of a head. Curling hair and a long twirling mustache appeared along with a face that she'd just been looking at.

The face of the original ringmaster, Eduardo De Rossi.

But he was dead.

He'd died a long time ago, and while planodiume could stop people from aging, surely it couldn't bring someone back from the—

Spectral transference's different. That's what Peter

Gallagher had said. *It's alive, and once it's transferred, all that energy has to go somewhere.*

Was someone trying to bring Eduardo De Rossi back to life?

Midnight's head spun. This was like nothing she'd dealt with before. In the past, the spectral energy had been trapped in some kind of object, or a person was using it to give themselves power. But this was worse.

I need to stop it.

She swung her backpack off her shoulder and fumbled for CARA. She'd done this a hundred times before, but it was the first time she'd ever used one of her weapons against spectral transference.

She braced her shoulder for the recoil and eased her finger down against the cool brass button. A burst of bright-white sparks shot out of the nozzle and hurtled toward the middle of the room.

The sparks encircled the glowing golden figure, and Midnight caught her breath at what was to come. But the sparks melted on impact and fell harmlessly to the ground.

It hadn't worked.

She pressed the button again, but the white burst of sparks didn't even reach the figure before it faded away. She rubbed her chin, trying to think, but her concentration was broken as the lights flickered.

A sharp buzzing hit her ears, and flashes of burning golden mist burst into the tent. The flashes ricocheted around the tent before darting into the prostrate glowing body on the table.

No.

Midnight instinctively aimed CARA at the raging golden light, but her fingers froze as an ear-shattering roar filled the room. It was followed by a throaty snarl that reverberated down her spine. She didn't want to look. Didn't want to move. All she wanted was to sink into her own bed and pull a comforter over her head.

But that wasn't an option. She dragged her reluctant gaze around to the large cage. In it was a lion.

The hair on the back of her neck prickled, and her heart pounded.

It roared again. Its sharp teeth flashed white as it raised a paw to try to smash open the grate.

Midnight was too terrified to scream as a second lion

appeared in a nearby cage. It also let out a thundering growl and dragged its claws along the wooden base.

Dissonant music flooded the room, and lights flashed and flickered. Everywhere she looked, more animals appeared, their eyes a blaze of golden fury.

Pale-pink fog danced in front of her, and her legs finally began to work.

She thrust her weapon away and followed Eliza as the cacophony of predatory roars chased after her. She ignored them, sprinted back down the twisting and turning corridor.

Wind whipped her hair in her eyes, and it was as if dark fingers were trying to drag her back into the tent. Panic caught in her throat, but she ran until she finally reached the purple flap and blinked as bright sunshine greeted her.

Tabitha and Logan rushed to her side as she leaned forward, trying to catch her breath.

It was several minutes before she could even stand up.

"Are you okay? What happened? We've been worried sick." Tabitha's words came out in a tumble, and her usually cool, calm demeanor was panicked.

"It's not good." Midnight hugged her arms, letting the warmth of the sun push away the darkness of the tent. She steadied herself and told them what had happened. She was shaking by the time she'd finished.

"Lions?" Tabitha's voice was little above a whisper. "As in real lions?"

Midnight nodded. "Whoever's stealing the spectral energy has figured out a way to conjure things up. I was so scared, I couldn't even move my finger."

"Whatever they're made from, it's obvious what they're doing there. Guarding Eduardo De Rossi," Tabitha said.

"They did a very good job of it," Midnight said. "Oh, and CARA didn't work. In fact, it made things worse, because as soon as I pressed the trigger, the menagerie woke up and started to attack me. Which means we need to find another way to stop them."

"We'll figure it out. We always do," Tabitha insisted before narrowing her eyes. "What's in your hand?"

"Oh." Midnight opened her palm to the crumpled piece of paper. "I forgot I had it. Eliza led me to it under the table. But then the lights went dark and the lion roared."

"It looks like a letter," Logan said quickly, as if not wanting her to relive what she'd just seen. That made two of them.

"Let's see what it says." Tabitha took it from Midnight's hand and flattened it out. They stared at the flowing cursive. "Dated the tenth of July eighteen ninety-nine. That's the day before Eduardo De Rossi died."

They didn't bother to ask how Tabitha knew the date of his death. Instead Midnight coughed and read it out loud.

"To the Bearer of This Letter,

I, Eduardo De Rossi, leave you my legacy. I am the greatest showman the world has ever seen and have dedicated my life to perfecting the true magic. Not for me some sleight of hand or tawdry back-alley deception. I'm talking about real magic. Made from the fabric of the world! Which is why I don't fear death—because I know it's not eternal.

If you've found this letter, then you've found my journal. Everything you need to help me return to life is there. It will show you how to get more power than you ever dreamed possible. Use it to bring me back to life, and I will share with you the final secret. A way to have everything you've ever dreamed about.

Until we meet again,

Yours, etc.

Eduardo De Rossi."

"Someone's trying to bring him back to life by using spectral transference. And they're using his journal to do it." Logan whistled.

"I can't believe we're up against a planodiume-powered dead ringmaster with a menagerie of animals. It's the stuff of bad horror movies," Midnight said, still trying to shake the overwhelming chaos from her mind.

"Did you see a journal when you found the letter?" Logan asked her.

"No." Midnight's head began to pound.

"The way I see it, we have two problems." Tabitha studied the letter. "We need to figure out how to get past Eduardo De Rossi's circus guards, and release the spectral energy so that it's returned to the victims."

"Actually." Logan coughed, his voice grave. "There's a third problem."

"Like what?" Tabitha's brows knitted together.

"Like the fact the tent's gone," Logan said.

"What?" Midnight and Tabitha yelled in unison. They turned around to find a food truck selling popcorn and sodas, with an overflowing trash can next to it. Impossible. Midnight took off her glasses and then slid them on again, but nothing changed. The faded purple tent that she'd just come out of was gone.

As if it had never been there.

She stepped back to where the doorway had been and pressed her hand out, trying to feel for it. Still nothing.

Logan was right.

They'd been so busy talking that none of them had seen the tent disappear. Yet, it was most definitely gone.

And worse. It wasn't just the tent that had vanished; it was also the floating body of Eduardo De Rossi.

CHAPTER SEVEN

"You look tired." Midnight's mom glanced up from the many scraps of paper she used for her to-do lists. "Don't tell me Rita kept you up."

If only.

But it wasn't the puppy that'd disrupted her sleep; it was the lions that had been guarding the floating body of Eduardo De Rossi.

Every time Midnight closed her eyes, the shattering roars pierced her brain, while dark shadows seemed to move against the bedroom walls, leaving her shaking and very, very wide awake.

What did it mean?

And where was the tent?

Or the journal. If they could find either of those things, they would have a chance to stop whoever was stealing spectral energy, before it was too late. But that was easier said than done.

Midnight, Tabitha, and Logan had spent the previous afternoon looking for the purple tent. They'd asked people who worked at the circus and had combed the fairgrounds searching for any sign of it. But they'd found nothing and had wound up with very sore feet.

"I'm fine." Midnight shuffled over and filled a bowl with some of her mom's homemade granola, hoping food would help her feel less tired.

"If you're up to it, I thought you and Taylor could drive over to the dog park on the other side of town. Phil researched it last night. There's a special part just for puppies. Rita will love it."

"Rita loves everything," Taylor corrected as she wandered in, the little puppy trailing behind her. "She loves boxes, her tail, my favorite Twenty One Pilots T-shirt, Phil's tennis racquet, and toilet paper. Besides, why does she need a puppy park when she has a perfectly good backyard to run around in?"

"I just thought it would be a nice change," their mom said, though Midnight suspected she was referring to Taylor, not Rita. "She loves having a walk."

At the mention of a walk, the small puppy ran around in a circle three times before running over to the door where her leash was coiled on the floor. She started to bark at it, using her paw to nudge it toward Taylor.

"Seriously, Mom? You had to say the *W* word?" Taylor folded her arms.

"It will do you both good. Besides, Phil and I are inter-viewing staff for the café all day, so you can take the car."

"I'll pass, thanks. I've got some reading to catch up on," Taylor said in a light voice, though her hands were clenched. Then she headed back upstairs, quickly fol-lowed by Rita who'd only stopped her barking so she could bite the leash and drag it along as she raced to keep up with Taylor.

"Since when does my seventeen-year-old daughter turn down a chance to drive my car?" Her mom frowned.

"It must be a pretty good book," Midnight said, just

as her phone rang. Peter's name flashed on the screen. Relief flooded her. She'd sent him a full report of what had happened in the tent yesterday, but she hadn't had a response. "It's a babysitting job. I'd better take it. Don't worry about Taylor. I'm sure she'll want to go to the park later this week."

"I hope you're right." Her mom sighed as Midnight hurried out of the kitchen and up the stairs into the safety of her own room.

"I'm not going to lie," Peter Gallagher said. "We're very concerned. There's never been a reported case of someone using spectral transference to bring back the dead. And to have the energy to also create a roomful of planodiume-charged animals is unprecedented. Not to mention being able to conceal the tent."

"Oh." Midnight sat down on the bed. It was worse than she'd thought. "Will you send someone else in?"

"I wish that were an option. But right now we're dealing with three Afterglow fractures, and a Black Stream in Thailand has been drained," he said. "Here's what we know. To transfer energy into another person, living or dead, they'd need a relic. Something personal that belonged to the person they're trying to resurrect. It's the relic that's used to store planodiume. Stopping it is just a matter of destroying the relic while it's in the presence of the person receiving the transference. This will send the stolen energy back to the victims."

Why did Midnight get the feeling that would be harder than it sounded?

"Destroy it with *what*?"

"Ah. We have a theory that one of the weapons we sent you last month should work. It's a small black box that fits onto a brass cylinder."

"Rockstar?" Midnight pulled the suitcase out from under her bed. She opened it and flipped away the heavy blanket she'd used to hide everything. Not that her mom would ever snoop, but it wasn't worth taking the chance.

Midnight lifted out the small device. The box had latticework across the front with black mesh peeking through underneath. Tabitha said it looked like a guitar amplifier.

"You named it?" Peter didn't sound amused.

"Sorry," Midnight said as she followed his instructions

and snapped the cylinder onto the side of the device. There was also a slender nozzle and a shoulder strap to make it easier to carry. It wasn't nearly as impressive as some of her other weapons. She wrinkled her nose. "Will this really work?"

"It's dual purpose. A carbonic resonator *and* something that can be used against spectral transference. Though we've never had a chance to test it. So, again, you'll be going into this blind."

"Okay." Midnight tried to remind herself that all the other weapons from the Agency had worked. "Once we find the tent, hopefully the relic will be inside. After all, there was loads of things in there. I'll just destroy them all until we figure out which is the relic."

"Good. I'll forward all the research we have. And, Midnight—"

"I know," she said. "Be careful."

He let out a reluctant laugh, but it did nothing to hide his concern. Before Midnight could ponder too much, Rita barked. A moment later, Tabitha's and Logan's voices sounded out as they walked up the stairs.

Midnight told them what Peter had said about the

relic, and then she packed Rockstar into her backpack. At least it didn't weigh as much as some of her other weapons. The plan was to catch a bus back to the circus. They *had* to find that tent. It seemed like the only thing that would lead them to the journal or the relic.

* * *

"All of me hurts," Tabitha complained later that afternoon as she rubbed her feet. "And I'm covered in dust. Since when are circuses so dusty?"

"Since we walked around it five times looking for an invisible tent." Midnight held a cold water bottle up to her forehead. Even Logan seemed despondent. She couldn't blame him.

"I've heard carnival people keep to themselves and don't trust outsiders, but I was sure that someone would give us a clue," he said. "Instead they looked at us as though we had some kind of disease."

"At least we have a weapon, so we're prepared," Midnight said, trying to lift the mood.

"It's not the most convincing weapon." Logan glanced to her backpack.

"Hey, Rockstar won't let us down," Tabitha defended.

"Of course, until we find the relic, we won't know for sure."

The three friends were silent as they sat in Tabitha's bedroom. Logan lived next door, but his house wasn't a safe place to talk, since Bella was always trying to sneak into the room. Midnight's house was equally bad, with the chaos of a small puppy and her mom's café preparations, not to mention the fire pit Phil was building for a summer solstice party.

Plus, Tabitha's mom made great snacks.

Midnight reached for a cookie and chewed it as Tabitha flipped open her MacBook, her fingers flying across the keyboard.

"I'm going to keep researching Eduardo De Rossi. See if I missed anything that might lead us to the relic," her friend said as Logan walked over to the whiteboard he loved to use.

"Good idea." He pulled the cap off a marker, his face thoughtful. "I'm going to mind map all the clues we have so far. Then we can start making a list of suspects."

And I'm sitting here eating a cookie.

Midnight gave her friends a guilty look as she straightened up and crossed her legs.

"I'll start researching if there are any other accounts of a phantom circus." She wiped away the cookie crumbs and opened her own laptop, and they all got to work.

Half an hour later, Tabitha looked up and grinned, her black and blue-streaked hair hanging over her shoulders. "Come and see what I've found. It's from an article in the *Berry Gazette* dated eighteen ninety-seven."

Midnight and Logan hurried over to read the scanned newspaper article up on the screen.

Circus Owner Dead!

Legendary magician Eduardo De Rossi seemed to have a Midas touch. Not only did his skills rival Harry Houdini's, but all the acts at his circus appeared to take on almost supernatural abilities.

But De Rossi's flamboyant career was also checkered with accidents and injuries to his employees and the patrons that visited his show.

It came to a head last week when twins Sarah and Samuel Vaughan, aged eight, were found mysteriously dead in the big top with no visible signs of injury. The twins' father, Alfred Vaughan, incited an angry mob who descended on the circus to demand answers. De Rossi was killed in the ensuing fight, and the circus left the following day, bringing to a close the tragic events that have marred our beloved town.

Logan let out a long whistle. "So, that explains Eduardo's promise in the letter. He obviously used planodiume to make his circus magnificent."

"Here's some more." Tabitha brought up another screen on her laptop. "Eduardo was very close to his father, Antonio, and was devastated when he died. He strongly believed that his father's magical abilities were underrated and was determined to make Cirque Fantastic a household name to honor him.

"After Eduardo's death, the circus was taken over by his wife until his young son Tony came of age. From Tony, it was passed to his son Giovanni, and then to Carlo."

Logan tapped at his mind map. He'd written up all the clues they had and circled them, then used lines to see what connections there were. And right in the middle of the board was the name Carlo De Rossi, the present-day ringmaster.

"You guessed it was him all along," Midnight said, but Logan shook his head.

"I didn't guess. I just went through the evidence. He owns the circus so he has the most to gain by making it great again. Plus, he's the most obvious person to have found Eduardo's letter and the journal. And there's something else. Remember that when we spoke to him, he said he wished Eduardo was here to help him."

"Whoa," said Tabitha. "He literally meant he wanted to bring him back to life."

It all seemed clear to Midnight, though it was still unsettling. On the surface, Carlo had been nice. Normal, even. Yet underneath he'd been stealing life from the general public, and from people like Joseph. People who were meant to be his friends.

"So tomorrow we follow Carlo and look for proof. See if we can find the journal, which would link him to what's been happening," Tabitha said.

Midnight rubbed her chin. "And we can also use our Pings to measure him. If he's working on Eduardo's behalf, it makes sense that he wouldn't have lost any of his own spectral energy. We should get a full reading from him."

"The only problem is how to get near him. If he suspects we're on to him, it might be harder to get close, let alone search his trailer," Logan said.

"We'll figure something out," Tabitha said in a confident voice.

"Agreed." Logan nodded, and they returned to their research. His dark hair flopped over one eye, and once again Midnight wished they could just be having a regular summer break, filled with suntan lotion, soda, and decisions about which movie to see. Instead, they were stuck with someone stealing life from unsuspecting people.

Midnight shook it off. As much as she wanted to think about Logan—and kiss him—she couldn't. She *wasn't* a regular girl.

Her job *had* to come first.

She'd turned back to her laptop to start researching when her Ping sang out.

It was followed a moment later by Tabitha's and Logan's Pings. They all reached for their devices and simultaneously studied the screens.

Midnight let out the breath she didn't know she was holding. "It's not at the circus. It's on the other side of town at Dingle Donuts."

"The Pings haven't been working for the spectral transference, which hopefully means this is just regular planodiume. No time-stealing golden lights," Logan said.

"What's the plan? Should we all go?" Tabitha wrinkled her nose.

"I can handle it," Midnight said reluctantly. Since Logan had joined the team, the three of them had often gone out on routine jobs together, and it had been fun. But right now it wasn't about fun. It was about getting to the bottom of the case as quickly as possible. Besides, Tabitha was always happiest when she was researching, and Logan had the amazing ability to look at clues like jigsaw puzzles and figure out how they all fit together.

Midnight gathered up her backpack, which was ready for any emergency. She called a cab and headed outside to wait for it.

Twenty minutes later, she was standing in front of Dingle Donuts. The place was famous for its jelly doughnut specials and the large, slowly turning fiberglass doughnut mounted on a pole on the roof of the building. But as Midnight looked up, the relentless buzz jangling in her ears, the giant doughnut was barely visible below the flickering black tendrils of trapped spectral energy.

She frowned.

The good news was that the energy wasn't anything like the golden light she'd seen in the big top.

The bad news was it was always more difficult to release spectral energy during the day when there were people around. Mainly because if they saw a twelve-year-old girl holding on to a weapon that looked like a cross between a trumpet and a Nerf gun, they'd probably have questions.

Questions she couldn't answer. Not without appearing to be a crazy person.

Midnight zeroed in on several dumpsters at the back of the parking lot, flanked by a brick wall. The setup wasn't ideal, but the long shadows that fell from the wall would give her a bit of cover. She hurried over and dropped to her knees.

There were several large boxes near the dumpster that she used to build a small fort. She unpacked CARA and checked that all the levels were set before holding the device just above the boxes. Her finger hovered over the brass lever, but before she could press it, the tinkling sound of shattered glass filled the air, followed by the incessant wail of a car alarm.

Her brow throbbed with the combined noise of the alarm and the spectral energy. Several people who'd been sitting outside the doughnut store ran toward a black Ford at the far end of the parking lot. It was a blessing in disguise.

If they were looking at the car, they wouldn't notice her.

She pressed down on the lever, bracing herself for the kickback of the weapon. Familiar pain ricocheted against her shoulder as brilliant white light poured out toward the rotating doughnut. The spectral energy howled in annoyance as it was dragged toward CARA.

It let out an ear-shattering cry, and the darkness was replaced by thousands of tiny rainbow-colored particles that spiraled up to the Afterglow.

Midnight sagged back against the dumpster, her breath ragged. It never ceased to amaze her how beautiful spectral energy was when it wasn't trapped and forced into its darker shadow self. When it was in its true form, being what it was meant to be.

Once the energy was gone, she packed CARA away. When she was back in the safety of her bedroom, she'd clean the weapon properly. But for now she just needed it out of sight.

She unsteadily got to her feet and slung her backpack over her shoulder, pretending it didn't weigh more than an elephant as she glanced over at the Ford. The alarm was still blaring as a police siren whirred in the distance.

She recalled what Phil had told her.

There've been a lot of car thefts lately.

Is that what'd happened here?

Then she shook her head. She could hardly handle the problems she had. And that was *with* her spreadsheet. Thinking about why so many cars were getting broken into wasn't something she had time for.

She walked back into the sunshine. A hunched figure was standing near the doughnut store, staring over at the crowd that'd gathered around the targeted Ford.

The person was wearing a dark hoodie, but it was impossible to miss the long, blond hair poking out. Midnight blinked.

Tyson Carl. Tabitha's boyfriend and Logan's best

friend. Who was supposed to be at his grandmother's house until Friday!

Midnight swallowed hard as her brain searched for a reason he could possibly be there. And why he'd lied about what he was doing. Should she go and talk to him? Ask him what was going on? Before she could decide, her phone rang.

"Hey," Tabitha said from down the other end. "How did it go? Any problems?"

Define "problems."

"Er, no. It's fine. It was in the giant doughnut on the roof, but I managed to hide behind a dumpster," she said as Tyson walked away from the store toward the bus stop.

"No way. That doughnut's been there my whole life. I'm glad it's okay."

"It'll live to spin another day," Midnight quipped before tightening her grip on the phone. It wasn't right to say she'd seen Tyson without knowing what he was actually doing. "How did the research go? Did you find anything?"

"Did I ever. Logan had to babysit Bella so I decided to go down to the cemetery and check out the De Rossi family gravestone again. Guess what I found."

"Dead flowers and weeds?" Midnight offered, but Tabitha wasn't amused.

"The Berry Cemetery Committee makes sure all the graves are cared for. This was way better. The gravestone has a stone snake wrapped around the top, which totally fits with what Joseph told us."

"A snake?" Midnight stiffened. "You think Carlo is using a snake as a relic?"

"Not a real snake," Tabitha quickly said. "It has to be an inanimate object, so it could be something in the shape of a snake, or with a snake emblem on it. If there's a snake on Eduardo De Rossi's gravestone, surely he had something else with a snake on it when he was alive."

"Okay." Midnight slowly nodded. "So now we just have one problem to worry about. How to find this snake thing."

"Actually." Tabitha coughed as if she was considering her words carefully. That couldn't be a good sign. "I've figured out a way to get the people at the circus to talk to us."

"That's great," Midnight said before frowning. "So, why don't you sound happy about it?"

"Because you're not going to like it. I don't like it either. But right now it's our best option."

"Okay," Midnight said in a cautious voice. "What is it?"

"My dad said that some of the local people who'd been hired by the circus have refused to go back. They think the accident was scary and that the circus might be haunted."

"And that means…?" Midnight asked.

"And that means the circus needs people for their cleanup crew, so Carlo is desperate. Long story short, the three of us are now officially employed by Cirque Fantastic. Which means we can snoop as much as we want."

"Tab, that's amazing," Midnight said before her eyes narrowed. "So, why don't you sound happy?"

"There's just one tiny thing I haven't mentioned yet," Tabitha said in a miserable voice. "There's a uniform. And it's kind of terrible…"

CHAPTER EIGHT

When Midnight had agreed to work with the Agency of Spectral Protection to keep the world safe, she knew the job involved risks—dangerous, terrifying, hideous risks. But nowhere was there any mention of wearing bright-green polyester coveralls.

"It's not that bad," her mom said in a valiant voice as she fiddled with the collar. It made absolutely no difference. The outfit still looked like something Kermit the Frog had once owned. Definitely a career low point.

"Mom's right." Taylor 2.0 bit back a smile, though Midnight could see the amusement in her sister's eyes.

Not that she could blame her. It really was a terrible uniform. Not to mention miles too big.

Still, that was the least of her worries.

"Just let me tack up the legs." Her mom took some safety pins and lowered herself to the ground while Rita ran around the kitchen, a blur of black-and-white fur. "There, that's—"

"Do not say 'better,'" Midnight warned as Tabitha trudged through the door looking equally green.

"Hey, everyone." Tabitha winced, probably allergic to wearing any color that wasn't black. "You ready to go?"

"Ready as I'll ever be." Midnight scooped up her backpack and said goodbye to her mom and sister before heading outside. "I still can't believe we're doing this."

"Makes two of us." Tabitha covered her eyes with sunglasses, and Midnight put her dark lenses over the top of her regular glasses. It wouldn't help them blend in, but it might stop them from being recognized as they walked to the bus stop.

"How did you do with your research last night?"

"Actually, Tyson invited me to the movies," Tabitha replied.

"Oh…I thought he was at his grandmother's house for a couple of days," Midnight said, suddenly remembering what she'd seen at Dingle Donuts.

"He was. But he got home at six and called me," Tabitha said, her face getting redder. "I hope you're not mad."

"No." Midnight quickly shook her head, still unsure if she should tell Tabitha what she'd seen. "Did you have fun?"

"It was really good. We went to a horror movie, and he liked it almost as much as I did."

"Great," Midnight said, even though she didn't quite share her friend's love of scary movies.

When their bus reached the circus, it didn't take long for Midnight to find Logan waiting for them in the crowds. Then again, in a frog-green uniform, he was hard to miss. Yet somehow he still looked amazing.

"I'm pretty sure Sherlock Holmes never went through this." He pushed a hand through his dark curls and gave the girls a rueful smile.

"Could be worse. When we went undercover at the country club a few months ago, I had to wear a tennis outfit. *A white one*," Tabitha said, shuddering. Then she collected herself. "Okay, so we all know the plan. We need to trail Carlo so he can lead us to the tent. And we need to search his trailer."

"And don't forget to look for anything marked with a snake," Midnight said.

"Or to get a Ping reading," Logan added. Then they smiled at each other and walked to the small office to report in for their first shift as cleaners.

* * *

Two hours later, Midnight's back was aching. Who knew collecting trash could be so exhausting? She wiped away small beads of sweat and checked her phone. No new messages. Tabitha and Logan had been sent to work in different parts of the circus, but they'd kept in touch by text.

None of them had found any new clues. Just lots and lots of trash. She was picking up a discarded soda can when out of the corner of her eye she saw a familiar figure walk by.

Carlo.

Midnight quickly checked to make sure that Ryan, her supervisor, wasn't around. She dumped the large bag she'd been using to collect trash and clutched at the second one she'd been carrying. The one that had her backpack in it.

She slung it over her shoulder as Carlo walked to the bumper cars, stopping on the way to smile and wave at the public.

Will he lead me to the purple tent?

His dazzling smile was brighter than ever. He stopped to talk to a woman holding a small baby and laughed as if he didn't have a care in the world.

Annoyance swirled in Midnight's stomach. She retrieved her Ping as Carlo continued over to a stall filled with helium balloons.

While Carlo was talking to the vendor, Midnight inched toward him. *Ping. Ping. Ping.* She looked at the screen, but Carlo still wasn't in range. She winced. If the reading said he hadn't lost any spectral energy, it would help prove he was behind the scheme to bring Eduardo back to life.

She reset her device and took a step closer just as Carlo abruptly turned and walked away. As she straightened up to follow him, she nearly collided with her supervisor. Ryan had a thin mustache and a giraffe-like neck. He was holding a wilted bunch of flowers and didn't look happy.

"Oh." She quickly slipped the Ping device back into her pocket. "H-hi."

"Midnight, is it?" The head cleaner lowered his neck to read her name badge. "Perhaps you'd care to explain why you're in the tenth quadrant when I'd clearly said you're working the third quadrant between hot drinks and the hammer-throwing ring," he said, referring to the color-coded map he'd handed out to all the staff. Usually she was a fan of such detailed organization. Today, not so much.

"Um, I saw someone dropping a whole bag of chips on the ground. Only feet from the bin," she improvised, desperately trying to search for Carlo, who'd melted away into the crowd.

Ryan was silent for a moment before giving her a curt nod.

"In the future, leave the vigilante work to me, understood?"

"Yes." She let out a breath.

"Good." He thrust the wilted flowers at her. "I need you to take these to a staff trailer. There should be a vase on the shelf. Make sure they have some water, and you can also wipe down the surfaces. It's a welcome home surprise for a performer who broke his leg."

"Joseph's being released from the hospital?" She tried to swallow her frustration at having to run errands instead of following Carlo. Ryan gave her a sharp look, as if surprised she knew the clown's name.

"That's right. And make sure you're back in your quadrant in ten minutes. That trash isn't going to pick up itself. Oh, and you'll need this. It's a master key to all the trailers." He handed her an inauspicious key.

The sweet perfume from the flowers caught in her nose, but she hardly noticed as her fingers tightened around the key. If it was a master one, it would also open Carlo's trailer. It was the break they needed.

"Nice work," Logan said five minutes later as they stood in a huddle outside the silver trailer. The place was all but deserted, thanks to the matinee performance that kept the crowds in the big top. Midnight had sent her friends a text as soon as Ryan had left. "I'll go keep an eye on Carlo and try to get a Ping reading. Then Tabitha can search his trailer while Midnight drops off the flowers."

"Shouldn't I help Tabitha?" Midnight asked. It'd been a frustrating morning, and she was itching to find the evidence they needed.

"I think it's safer if at least one of us is where we're meant to be," Tabitha said. "If Ryan goes to Joseph's trailer and you're not there, he might come looking for you."

"I guess." Midnight reluctantly nodded as Logan hurried off to the big top. Tabitha used the master key to open Carlo's trailer, then handed it back.

"I'd better get started. I'll text you as soon as I find anything." Her friend's eyes were full of sympathy. "I promise I'll search everywhere."

"I know you will," Midnight said before walking toward the clown's trailer.

Unlike Carlo's modern Winnebago, Joseph's mobile home was like something from the previous century—all wood with red and yellow trim. She unlocked the door and stepped inside.

There was a curtained-off area that must be the

bedroom, a small table under the window, and a tiny kitchen built into the wall.

It didn't take Midnight long to find a vase and fill it with water. She tried to display the flowers as best she could. Then she searched for a cloth to clean the surfaces. There wasn't much to wipe. As well as the bench and table, there was a tiny television sitting on top of a bookshelf, filled with a collection of tattered paperbacks. For someone who prided themselves on not reading, Joseph sure had a lot of books.

Once she finished, Midnight quickly locked up the mobile home and hurried back to Carlo's trailer to help Tabitha. Her friend was waiting under the awning, her mouth set in an apologetic line.

"Nothing. I was so sure I'd find a clue," Tabitha said just as Logan reappeared, shaking his head.

"I've got bad news. I got close enough to Carlo to get a reading. It doesn't look good."

"What do you mean?" Tabitha asked as he held up his Ping so they could see the results.

SED: 20.05%
Life-Span Depletion: 5.13 years.

"Five years? Someone's stolen *five years* of his life?"

The words echoed out as the three friends stared at each other. There was no way Carlo was the person they were looking for. Which meant they were back to square one.

CHAPTER NINE

"This is where the tables will go." Midnight's mom pointed to a space currently stacked high with boxes of glasses and plates. The café was in an older part of town, so the decor made the space feel like a time capsule. And since it had previously been a burger joint, a bakery, and an electronics store, there was a lot of work to be done.

"It'll look better once the walls aren't fluorescent green." Phil appeared from the half-built kitchen. He was wearing white overalls and holding a large bucket of paint and a roller in his hands.

Midnight noticed another paint roller lying nearby,

waiting to be used, but she tried to ignore it. Painting the café was the last thing she wanted to be doing.

"Oh, and this arrived for you this morning." Her mom handed her a padded envelope. "It's from England. It says on the back it's from a book club."

"Thanks," Midnight said, taking the parcel. It definitely felt book-shaped, but this was one of the ways ASP sent her equipment without raising suspicion. "I won an online quiz."

"Lucky you," her mom said. "Aren't you going to open it?"

Thankfully Midnight was saved from answering as Rita charged in, sniffing at everything in her path. Taylor was at the other end of the puppy's leash.

"At least someone's happy to be here," her sister murmured as she reluctantly picked up the little dog before she could lick a dirty cloth. "I hate painting, so I'll start cleaning the kitchen."

An hour later, Midnight stepped back to inspect her handiwork. The wall still glowed like something from a lab experiment. At this rate, she'd probably need to paint it about fifty-seven times.

"You girls are doing a great job," her mom said, a smudge of paint on her nose as Phil walked in with two pizzas from the store up the road. Taylor appeared from the kitchen, a surprised expression on her face.

"You bought Mama J's?" Her sister arched an eyebrow, much like Midnight had done with the surprise trip to Cookies and Cakes. Their mom was as transparent as a window. "What's going on?"

"Does there need to be a reason for pizza?" Phil said in a light voice.

"You're opening a vegan café and buying me a double cheese pizza. So, yeah." Taylor folded her arms.

"It's not like that," their mom said, a guilty flush stealing up her neck. "I just thought it'd be nice. Also, it's a good chance to chat about summer jobs. I could call John Wilson and see if he could get you one at the circus."

"What?" Midnight yelped. While she knew her mom and Phil were just trying to get Taylor to leave the house, sending her to work at the circus—a place filled with supernatural danger—wasn't exactly a good idea. Especially since it was the kind of danger that had freaked her sister out in the first place. "Er, I mean if Taylor got a job at the circus, how could she look after Rita?"

"I'm sure Maggie and I can manage one little puppy." Phil flipped open the pizza box, and the room filled with the smell of mozzarella and rich, spicy tomatoes.

"It could be fun," their mom added.

Taylor blinked. "You think it would be fun to collect trash for eight hours? Besides, I need to prepare for my junior year. I have reading to do. You're the one telling me to get a good education."

"I'm worried about you. You haven't driven the car in a month. It's like you're becoming a hermit."

"I like to think that I'm saving the environment by not using so much gas. Is that so bad?"

Crash.

The tinkling of broken glass filled the room as a large box toppled over and fell to the floor, in turn knocking over the bucket of paint. They all stared helplessly as white paint sluggishly spread across the wooden floor in slow motion.

Rita broke the silence as she darted away from the box and hid under a painting sheet, black tail poking out.

"No!" Midnight's mom let out a little wail as she

walked to the fallen box. It rattled like a maraca when she picked it up. "Two dozen glasses and a gallon of paint."

"It's my fault. I should've put them behind the counter." Phil tried valiantly to stop the paint from spreading any farther while Midnight comforted the frightened puppy.

"It's okay," she crooned as Phil moved the boxes out of harm's way.

"Still want me to run away to the circus?" Taylor quirked an eyebrow.

Their mom let out a frustrated sigh. "It was just an idea. Now, who wants pizza?"

Midnight couldn't help but be relieved. Taylor working at the circus would mean one more thing to worry about, and right now Midnight had to focus on her research. Before anyone else had years of their life stolen from them.

* * *

"I want to make sure you all stick to your allocated quadrants." Ryan folded his arms, making the sleeves on his two-sizes-too-small uniform hike up over his wrists. Several cleaners let out a low groan. Midnight couldn't blame them. She was a big fan of structure, but Ryan's cleaning system felt more like prison work.

Her hand slipped into her pocket. Inside the book Peter had sent had been a small silver button. It was a locator device for when she found the tent. All she had to do was put the button on the tent, and then her friends would be able to find it using their Pings.

"What if we've finished cleaning our quadrant?" someone asked.

"Then you go back to the starting point and do it again. Trust me, it doesn't take these animals long to drop more corn dogs onto the ground," he growled. "Now, let's make this the cleanest place in Berry."

He punched his arm in the air as if to rally the troops, but was only answered in grunts as everyone retrieved their cleaning gear and walked outside.

"You know the drill," Tabitha said in a low voice as she sidled up next to Midnight. "Text if you find anything."

"Will do," she said, earning herself a dark look from Ryan.

She hurried over to Logan.

"It's okay," he murmured as if picking up on her anxiety.

"We're going to find our suspect today. I'm sure of it."

Midnight gave him a grateful smile, but before she could reply, Ryan appeared and pointed in the direction of the food trucks. She gritted her teeth and reminded herself to focus on the bigger picture.

* * *

"Finally." Tabitha let out a dramatic sigh as she turned in her shift log sheet and the three friends walked out of Ryan's office. "If I never see another piece of trash again, it'll still be way too soon. This was the worst idea ever."

"Is this where I point out that it was actually *your* idea?" Logan said, a half smile tugging at his mouth, making him look super cute.

"I wish you wouldn't," Tabitha said before letting out a groan. "Trouble at twelve o'clock."

"What?" Midnight followed Tabitha's gaze and stiffened.

It was Savannah Hanson and her sidekick, Lucy Sargent, who happened to have Midnight right at the top of their hate list. She'd been part of their group before discovering that some friendships weren't worth keeping.

Back when they were friends, Midnight had spent all her money on stylish outfits like theirs that left her feeling uncomfortable most of the time. She'd since discovered it was a lot easier to protect spectral energy when wearing jeans, a T-shirt, and a pair of sneakers.

She shuddered to think how they would've teased her if she'd ever told them about her ASP job.

The two girls stopped in the middle of the crowd, and Sav held up her phone as the pair of them pushed their lips into matching pouts and posed for a selfie.

"Should we avoid them?" Tabitha's voice was hopeful.

"Absolutely." Midnight glanced down at the green coveralls they were wearing. Not that she cared what her ex-friends thought, but still, it was a conversation she could do without. "Because the—"

She broke off as Sav held up her arm for another photo. Wrapped around her upper arm was a bracelet in the shape of a snake.

A golden snake.

Chapter Ten

"I know that look." Tabitha's voice was laced with concern as she studied Midnight's face. "What is it?"

"I think I've found a clue," Midnight admitted, still staring at the bracelet curling up Sav's arm.

Could that be the relic they were looking for?

"Where?" Tabitha said before her brows shot up. "No. No. No. Please tell me they're not the clue." Then she sighed as she finally seemed to notice Sav's arm bracelet. Lucy had a matching one.

"This is our first fresh lead. We need to find out where they got those bracelets," Logan said.

"See, this is why I prefer doing research and spending time in the cemetery," Tabitha grumbled.

"Tell me about it." Midnight sighed as they walked toward the two girls.

"Oh, look who it is," Savannah drawled. As always, her hair was in perfect waves of golden sunlight, while her outfit was straight out of a magazine. "The geek squad."

"I think you mean 'freak squad.'" Lucy snickered as she glanced at the green uniforms and then back to their red, sweating faces. She held up her phone and took a picture of them, her mouth smirking. "Like, seriously, what's wrong with you three? Oh, actually 'freak squad' is the perfect hashtag to go along with the picture."

"You wouldn't dare," Tabitha growled before Midnight elbowed her.

"It's a free country." Lucy tapped the post button and grinned. Tabitha glowered some more.

"Don't engage them. Their fashion sense might be contagious," Savannah stage-whispered while giving them a sweet-as-pie smile that didn't quite meet her eyes. "Now, if you don't mind, we have to go and meet someone who actually knows how to dress."

Midnight took a deep breath and swallowed down all the things she longed to say. Her job was to keep people safe. Even people like Sav and Lucy. And she couldn't do that without talking to them.

"Wait," Midnight said, which earned her a frosty glare from the two girls. She coughed and tried again. "So I really love those bracelets. Where did you get them?"

"Why?" Lucy folded her arms.

"Wouldn't you like to know," Tabitha retorted before seeming to catch the look Midnight shot her. "Er, because you both have such great taste."

"I think that's obvious." Sav gave a dismissive flick of her hair. "Since you're so interested, Zelda the Great gave them to us after she did a reading. They match the one she wears."

"A *very good* reading," Lucy interjected. "We're both going to meet a stranger with blue eyes."

"Gee, it sounds like true love," Tabitha retorted. This time Midnight didn't even try to stop her friend.

"You're a good one to talk." Sav glared. "And you might as well save yourself twenty bucks, because the only future you've got is as losers."

"Nice one." Lucy giggled on cue as the two girls linked arms and sauntered off toward the large carousel as if they were on a fashion runway rather than at a small-town carnival.

A haunted carnival at that.

"That was painful." Tabitha waited until the girls were out of hearing.

"So, do you think they were telling the truth about the bracelets?" Logan rubbed his chin.

"They don't have any reason to lie. And if Zelda has a snake bracelet, it could be the relic. After all, she'd want to keep it near her at all times to make sure it was safe," Tabitha said just as Midnight let out a soft gasp.

"Remember we saw Zelda at the hospital? I bet she was there to make sure Joseph didn't talk."

"She could've just been a concerned friend. We know how tight-knit carnival folks are. Besides, we have no proof." Logan frowned.

"Actually, I think we do." Tabitha's face was even whiter than usual as she held up her phone.

Her friend had done a quick online search and found Zelda's website. There were several photos of the fortune-teller, and in each one her left arm was exposed, showing a gleaming bracelet shaped like a golden snake.

Midnight turned toward the tent, but Logan caught her.

"I think we should do more research first. We don't know how dangerous she is."

"All the more reason to stop her," Midnight said, once again thinking of how her sister had been affected. Of how it might have been prevented if Midnight had figured everything out sooner. They couldn't afford to wait.

"I don't like it, but she's right," Tabitha said as Midnight slipped her backpack off her shoulder and set it on the ground to make sure Rockstar was all set up. "Be careful."

"I promise," she said, walking toward the tent.

Zelda was still sitting outside, and as they got closer, her eyes widened in recognition.

"Ah, you came back. I knew you would," the fortune-teller said, her heavy jewelry jangling as she beckoned Midnight toward her, while the golden snake seemed to slither up her arm.

Unlike the plastic ones Sav and Lucy had been wearing, this one had intricate scales carved into the precious metal, as well as two bright-green emeralds glittering where the eyes should be.

"Came back? What's she talking about?" Logan knit his brows together as if trying to figure out a puzzle.

"Nothing," Midnight quickly replied, not wanting to discuss her attempts to plan their first kiss. It seemed like a million years ago now. "I guess she's just proving that she really is psychic."

Midnight stepped forward, her knuckles white as they gripped her backpack. There hadn't been time to make a spreadsheet action plan.

"Come." Zelda opened the flap of the tent, gesturing for Midnight to follow.

The floor was covered with rich burgundy rugs, decorated with intricate patterns, while the walls were concealed by sheer pieces of purple and pink fabric, all trimmed with swirling silver patterns.

On a high chest was a large photograph that looked like it was a hundred years old. A woman almost identical to Zelda was standing next to a tall tree. At her feet was a coiled-up snake with eyes like diamonds.

Midnight shuddered.

"That's my great-great-grandmother. Our Romany gift has been passed down through eight generations."

"D-did she really have a snake?"

"Yes, she was as famous for charming as she was for seeing the future," Zelda explained, holding up her own arm. Then she winked. "But don't worry, these days I only use the cards and a crystal ball to pass on messages from the spirits."

"Oh." Midnight dragged her gaze away from the photograph. She found the heavy incense cloying as she breathed it in, and sweat beaded on her forehead.

Why had she ever thought this was a good idea?

"Sit down. Tell me what you'd like to know." Zelda pointed to a folding chair. It was next to a round table draped in shawls similar to the one Zelda was wearing. The woman lifted one off the tabletop to reveal a crystal ball underneath, as well as a pack of tarot cards. To the right was a bowl of plastic golden snake bracelets.

"I'm not here for a reading. I wanted to ask you a few questions."

"Ask whatever questions you want. The price is the same, and my answers always come from those who guide me."

Midnight handed over twenty dollars. Part of her wanted to ask for a receipt so she could claim the expense to the Agency, but the other part wanted to get out of there as quickly as possible.

"I'm looking for the purple tent."

"The tent?" Zelda stiffened, and the relaxed smile fell away. "Whatever you thought you saw, you were mistaken. Do you understand?"

So, it was true.

"You know what I'm talking about? You can see—"

"I see nothing." Zelda leaned forward, her fingers clamping down on Midnight's arm. Her touch was ice cold. A shudder went up Midnight's spine. "If you're smart, you'll not see it either."

Midnight snatched her arm away, visions of Joseph's blank expression as he fell to the ground still fresh in her mind. Of the golden figure of Eduardo De Rossi, slowly being brought back to life at the expense of other people. Of the cacophony of sounds made by the lions and elephants trying to get out of their cages. All snarling at her.

"No." Midnight slid her hand into her backpack, gripping the top of Rockstar. "It has to stop."

Zelda opened up her mouth, but no words came out. Then she snatched up Midnight's money and thrust it back at her.

"I can't help you." Zelda glanced around the tent as if fearful something was there. Spying on them. She lowered her voice. "If you walk this path, you'll end up all alone. Turn back while there's still time. You're not special, Midnight Reynolds."

"What?" Midnight said, just as the screeching sound of static rang in her ears.

Jagged shards of light swirled into the room and whipped around Zelda's body like a hurricane. The veils on the walls were blown into the air, and the crystal ball rocked back and forth on the wooden plinth in the center of the table.

The hiss of something cracking split the air, sharp and deadly.

A snake?

"Go," Zelda snarled before her eyes turned to gold and her face went slack. Then the golden light disappeared from the room as if it had been sucked away by a vacuum.

The fortune-teller crumpled to the ground, her skin slick with sweat.

"What's going on?" Midnight's friends burst into the tent.

Logan was holding his beloved notebook high above his head, and Tabitha had taken off one of her black studded boots, as if to hurl it.

"Are you okay?" Tabitha's gaze darted back and forth before settling on Zelda's crumpled figure. "Scrap that question."

"We need an ambulance." Midnight dropped to the ground and made sure the fortune-teller's airway was clear, grateful their gym teacher had spent so much time drilling them in first aid.

"I'll call my dad." Tabitha reached for her phone and had a short conversation before ending the call. "He'll be here in a couple of minutes with the medics. What happened?"

"Zelda's not the villain. She's another victim. It was the same light. Her eyes turned golden, and she collapsed." Midnight tried to ignore her shaking hands as she retrieved her Ping. "We need to get a reading before anyone arrives."

The device beeped, and Logan and Tabitha both leaned over her shoulder to study the screen.

Spectral Energy Levels: 19.04%

Life-Span Depletion: 4.8 years

"Almost five years? That's the same as Joseph." Logan's voice was hoarse.

"You need to leave." Zelda gasped, her voice faint. "It isn't safe here."

"Please, if you tell me what you know, I can stop it."

"I don't know anything." Zelda's mouth flattened, her voice like a recording.

"Look at her eyes. It's the same blank expression that everyone at the circus has had. I think whoever's responsible is somehow stopping people from talking about it," Logan said.

Using planodiume for mind control?

Midnight stiffened as the tent flap was dragged back and Tabitha's dad hurried in, closely followed by a medic.

"You kids did great. We can take over." He gave them a steady smile as the medic checked for vitals. "Why don't you three wait outside?"

Tabitha's face was pale, as if she was unsure about leaving her dad alone in a tent that had been filled with the golden light only moments earlier.

"We don't need to go. We can wait by the door," Midnight said in a low voice.

"Okay." Tabitha nodded, and the three of them trailed outside to where the fairground was still in full swing. Midnight blinked, trying to readjust to the light.

"What happened?" Logan's face was pinched. "Did you find out about the snake?"

"It was a false lead. The snake bracelet is because her great-great-grandmother was a snake charmer. It's got nothing to do with the case. Which means we still don't know what the relic is." Midnight shook her head and relayed the rest of the conversation, omitting the last part.

You're not special, Midnight Reynolds.

That wasn't true. She was special. That's why she could see spectral energy and why she could stop people from using planodiume.

Zelda was just trying to scare her off, but it wouldn't work.

CHAPTER ELEVEN

"Logan's right," Peter Gallagher said on the phone the following morning as Midnight climbed off the bus and walked toward Cookies and Cakes. She'd been waiting all evening for him to call her back, but he'd been dealing with a crisis. "About the mind control."

"Oh." Midnight stopped, causing someone behind her to mutter. An elderly man scowled as he walked around her. She mumbled an apology and sat down at the bus stop so she could pull out the spreadsheet she'd been working on. She quickly wrote the new clue into one of the cells along with a question mark. "What does that mean for us?"

"It means that whoever you're looking for is strong," Peter said. "Very strong. Using planodiume to wipe away people's memories and control what they say is highly dangerous, and…"

"And?" Midnight asked, all too familiar with how her boss worked. If he was pausing or lost for words, it could only mean one thing. The worst was yet to come.

"It also makes them unstable. Remember Dylan and Miss Appleby? The more planodiume they're exposed to, the more erratic they become."

"Which technically makes it easier for us to find them," Midnight said lightly, but Peter's voice remained grim.

"This is no joking matter. If they suspect you're after them, there's no saying what they might do. And if they succeed in bringing Eduardo De Rossi back to life, it's only the start. Who else might they bring back?"

Midnight gulped and looked at her spreadsheet. At the empty cells where evidence was meant to go. So far they had nothing, yet the stakes kept getting higher. If Peter was right, the villain could bring anyone back to life. And she doubted they would be playing for Team Good.

"What do you suggest?" she said, her throat tight.

"For a start, you can't trust what the circus folk tell you, because there is no way of knowing if they're being controlled. And don't go anywhere on your own. Make sure your friends know where you are at all times."

"Copy that," Midnight agreed, pushing down the memory of going into the purple tent on her own. Even going into Zelda's tent yesterday had left her drained and anxious. "At least the cleaning job lets us search without raising suspicions."

"It's an excellent cover," Peter Gallagher said as an alarm went off on his end of the line. He muttered something under his breath and then sighed. "Sorry, I have to take this. But I can't stress enough. The sooner you stop this person, the better."

"We will." She finished the call and stared at her spreadsheet. If they couldn't trust anything the people at the circus had told them, half their evidence wasn't valid. All they had now were the readings of the people who'd had time stolen from them, and what she'd seen and heard when Joseph and Zelda had been attacked. A golden light and a strange hissing noise that might or might not be a snake.

It wasn't a lot to go on.

Still, they were one step closer. Regardless of what Peter said, knowing the person they were looking for was unstable might make it easier to find them. Plus, if they could find Eduardo's journal, it would lead them to the relic.

Midnight packed away her laptop. It was only a short distance to Cookies and Cakes and she jogged, eager to give her friends an update.

Logan and Tabitha were sitting at their favorite table.

"I've just spoken to Peter," Midnight said without even saying hello. "And—"

"Oh, hey, Midnight. If I'd known you were here, I would've got you a soda." Tyson Carl appeared by her side holding a tray with three drinks. There was no sign of the black hoodie, and his straggly blond hair hung around his face as he gave her a friendly smile.

"H-hi, Tyson," she stammered. "Nice to see you."

"Ditto." He grinned and sat down. "Seems like ages since we've all hung out."

"The circus is keeping us busy. We should have some spare time soon," Logan said in a smooth voice while exchanging a smile with Midnight.

"Sounds good. By the way, how was your trip to the swimming pool last week?"

"We didn't make it," Logan said. "Something came up."

"That's too bad. We could always go tomorrow. I'm free all day. What do you guys say?"

The three friends were silent before Tabitha coughed. "We have to work tomorrow. Ryan was saying that he's never met bigger litterbugs than here in Berry."

A flash of hurt crossed Tyson's face, but a moment later it was gone. "Sure. That's cool."

"Trust me, even *I* would rather go to the swimming pool than collect trash," Tabitha said, and the next ten minutes were spent talking about their favorite YouTube clips before Tyson's phone beeped. He studied the screen and frowned.

"Sorry. I've gotta blaze." He gave Tabitha a shy smile before nodding to Midnight and Logan and hurrying out of the café. As soon as he was gone, Midnight let out her breath.

"I didn't know Tyson was going to be here. I almost blew our cover."

"We didn't either. He was here with his older sister, but when he saw us, he came to hang out," Tabitha explained.

"We've been so busy with the circus and working that I haven't seen much of him," Logan added.

Midnight's throat tightened. "Is everything okay? Are you mad that you've been helping me?"

"No." Tabitha quickly shook her head.

They spent the next hour going over everything Midnight had learned from Peter about mind control. Her friends agreed that they could no longer trust what anyone at the circus told them, which meant they were back to searching for the mysterious tent in the hope that whoever was stealing spectral energy from people would turn up there again.

Midnight was just packing away her laptop when Tabitha's mom sent a text. Her friend's face went pale as she read it out loud.

There's been another accident at the circus. On the Ghost Ride.

* * *

Midnight stood in front of the Amazing House of Horrors Ghost Ride half an hour later. Security tape had been set up to stop people from getting too close, but it hadn't prevented a crowd from forming.

The painted exterior resembled a haunted house with a broken wooden porch, and in front of it was a small metal track where three silver carriages were resting. She already knew that the track snaked along the front of the house and then swung around like a roller coaster as it ventured into the gloomy interior filled with fake ghosts and spiders.

Tabitha held her Ping up and pointed it in the direction of the same skinny guy who'd been working the ride the other day. He hadn't been injured, but he was sitting on the ground, looking perplexed. The device pinged, and they studied the reading.

SED: 12%

Life-Span Depletion: 1.3 years

"This is not good news." Logan ran a hand through his hair, frustration tugging at his mouth. "We don't know if it was all taken today or if it's been stolen a little bit at a time."

"And we can't ask him because he's probably been mind-controlled," Midnight added as Tabitha finished talking to her dad and returned. Her face was grim. That didn't bode well.

"Five people were injured and are on their way to the hospital," Tabitha said.

"We need to get readings from them." Midnight wrapped her arms around her chest. *And find the person responsible.*

"Agreed." Tabitha turned to Logan. "How do you feel about going to the hospital to see what you can find out?"

"Of course," Logan said. "Do you want to meet me there when you're finished here?"

"Definitely," Midnight said, and after saying goodbye to Logan, the two girls surveyed the area.

Carlo was talking to a couple of police officers while Ryan, the cleaning supervisor, stood off to the left. Midnight had to remind herself that she and Tabitha were off duty and didn't have to worry about getting in trouble if Ryan saw them. Still, she didn't want to chance him asking what they were doing. They headed toward the back of the ride. They found a single door for staff leading inside the House of Horrors. Midnight slipped her purple backpack off her shoulders so Rockstar would be close at hand as they stepped in.

The whole place was black, and Tabitha muttered as she flicked her flashlight app on. Cool steel tracks for the train ride were all around them, while the ghosts and ghouls designed to jump out and scare people lay hanging and dormant.

Without the creepy music and flashing lights, the House of Horrors was even less scary than when they'd been on the ride.

Tabitha poked her finger at a Victorian doll that was sitting on a fake gravestone with a knife in its hand. "It's like they're not even trying. I mean, they could've at least broken her neck to make her look creepy."

"There's been far too much creepy stuff lately. I can do without having to look at possessed dolls," Midnight whispered back. "And we'd better be quiet. If we're caught in here, it might tip off whoever we're looking for."

"Okay," Tabitha whispered, and they continued through the place, ducking to avoid the fake cobwebs that blocked the way. It took ten minutes before they ended up back where they'd started.

"Should we look some more?" Midnight asked just as the purr of engines caused the tracks to rumble. Carnival music flooded the area, and lights flickered on and off. The ride was being restarted. "I guess that answers the question."

"We'd better get out of here," Tabitha said as another light flickered and something on the ground glinted. "What's that?"

Midnight bent down, using her flashlight to examine the object. It was a thin strip of gold rope. It could have come from anywhere, like the tassel of a costume. Still, right now they were short on ideas, so she slipped it into one of the small plastic bags Logan insisted they all carry.

He'd wanted them to wear gloves as well, but since Tabitha had pointed out that it wasn't like spectral energy left behind fingerprints, contaminating evidence wasn't really a problem. Personally, Midnight thought it had been an adorable idea, since it showed how seriously he took the job.

She slipped the bag into her pocket, and they hurried for the door. Bright sunshine greeted them as they stepped outside.

"Ah, look who it is." A voice cut through her thoughts as Joseph the clown appeared next to them. "This is a surprise."

He could say that again.

Midnight swallowed. Joseph was wearing a pair of tracksuit pants and his leg cast was clearly visible as he leaned forward on his crutches. His fingers glittered with several gold rings, and a gold chain hung at his neck. It looked like he'd been raiding Zelda's jewelry collection.

His arm was still heavily bandaged, and he winced as he moved.

"Er, hi," Midnight quickly said, while Tabitha nodded in recognition. "We didn't expect to see you here. Is your leg okay?"

"No thanks to that hospital," he complained. "And the food they served—not that you can call it food. Cardboard would've tasted better. Still, it's good to be back. I hear you're working here now. I bet I can guess why."

"You can?" Tabitha's voice was hoarse.

"Well, yeah." He grinned with a wink. "You're still working on that English paper, aren't you? Not that this accident was as dramatic as mine, since there wasn't fire. Well, I'd better be on my way. Carlo has organized a surprise party for me. I don't want to be late."

"Wait. If it's a surprise, how do you know about it?"

Midnight wrinkled her nose.

He laughed. "You'd be amazed at what I know." Then without another word he swung himself around with the crutches and limped away. They waited until he was out of hearing range before turning back to each other.

"That was way too close," Midnight said.

"But it shows how awesome our original cover story was," Tabitha pointed out. "We didn't even have to explain why we were sneaking around in the House of Horrors ride. He just assumed it was for our English assignment."

"True. Though next time I could do without the stress," Midnight said as her phone dinged with a text message from her mom.

Something's come up. Can you please come and help at the café?

Midnight winced. She'd promised to meet Logan at the hospital. But if she said no to her mom, she might have to explain what she was doing instead. Which would mean either lying or telling the truth. Neither was a good option.

Okay. I'm on my way.

"Problem?" Tabitha said.

"I've been roped into helping at the café." Midnight sighed. "Do you mind meeting Logan on your own?"

"Don't hate me, but I can't. I told Tyson I'd hang out with him. I'm sure Logan won't mind."

"Of course." Midnight nodded. She felt bad that Logan was doing all the work at the hospital while she and Tabitha did other things. She quickly sent him a text message to say she was sorry they couldn't meet him. *See you tomorrow?* she typed. He replied a moment later with a smiley face.

"It's going to be okay," Tabitha said in a soft voice, as if sensing Midnight's panic. "It always is."

Midnight nodded and crossed her fingers.

Before she could brood too much, her phone rang. It was Peter Gallagher.

"I was just about to call you," Midnight said. "There's been another accident, and five people were injured. Logan's at the hospital trying to get some readings."

"I'm not surprised," Peter said in a worried voice. "We've just found something out. There's a reason the circus is back in Berry. The only way planodiume can bring someone back to life is if the ritual is completed at the same place as their death."

"What?" Midnight's head began to spin. "But the circus is only here for six more days."

"That's why you have to act quickly. Before things get worse."

CHAPTER TWELVE

"Since when do you walk so fast?" Midnight raced to keep up with her sister, who was jogging along behind Rita. Not that she wanted to be out walking when she could be poring over her spreadsheet. But her mom hadn't given her much choice: go with Taylor for a walk, or spend the morning cleaning the café before her circus shift in the afternoon.

It was obviously part of Operation Get Taylor Out of the House.

At least it was helping Midnight keep her mind off Logan. She'd left him several messages but hadn't heard back. She just had to hope he'd found something. And that he wasn't mad at them for abandoning him at the hospital.

"It's not me." Taylor took a gulp of her coffee as the puppy stopped to sniff a tree. "This dog has supernatural strength. The only good thing is I'll have killer abs by the time Rita's owner gets back from California next week."

"Plus you're getting paid," Midnight reminded her, still feeling guilty that Taylor had been stuck holding the doggy bone, so to speak.

"I am," Taylor said as Rita continued to investigate the grass at the base of the oak. "Though I'm pretty sure that's not the reason Mom made you come out with me."

Midnight sighed. "She's worried."

"Because I'm being a model teenage daughter who'd prefer to stay home rather than go out?" Her sister pressed her lips together as if considering her next words. "Did you tell her I'm fine?"

"I tried. But you know how good her radar is. She can figure these things out. Maybe you should go out with Donna. It might stop Mom from freaking."

"No," Taylor snapped before catching herself. "Donna's busy right now."

"Is everything okay with you two?"

Taylor uncharacteristically ran a hand through her long hair. "She's been hanging out with Libby Carl a lot."

"Tyson's older sister?" Midnight frowned.

"I know he's a friend of yours, and I'm sure he's a good kid, but his sister's wild. She and Donna have been going out a lot. To parties on the wrong side of town. Full of college kids, who are…well, who are doing things I don't want to do. After what happened with Dylan, I don't want to make any more bad decisions. Staying home is safest."

"I'm sorry," Midnight said truthfully. She couldn't imagine not having her friends around her. She was also trying hard not to think about Tyson's older sister being wild. Did that mean he was wild too?

It would explain what she'd seen at the parking lot.

"It's not your fault." Taylor shrugged.

"Is there anything I can do?"

"You've got enough on your plate," Taylor said as Rita let out a little bark and tugged at the leash again. They reluctantly resumed their jogging. "Speaking of… How's it going?"

"Not good." Midnight filled her sister in on the attack on Zelda as well as yesterday's accident on the ghost ride. Not to mention Peter's dire warning and the ticking clock they were up against.

"Is Zelda still in the hospital? And what about everyone else?" Taylor came to a halt, much to Rita's annoyance.

"Zelda was back telling fortunes yesterday," Midnight said. "And Logan was checking everyone at the hospital. I haven't heard from him yet. Don't worry, we'll get to the bottom of it. Even if I have to pick up every piece of trash in the circus."

"I believe you," Taylor said in a surprisingly fierce voice. "You and your friends make quite a team."

Midnight blinked at the compliment. Yes, she and her sister were getting along better than ever, but still, Taylor wasn't normally quite so generous with her words. Unbidden, Zelda's dire warning flashed into her mind. *You're not special, Midnight Reynolds.* She pushed it aside. Zelda might see the future, but that didn't mean she knew everything.

Midnight had stopped plenty of other things, and she'd stop this too.

Rita barked again as Tabitha walked toward them. Her black dress caught in the wind, and the blue streaks in her hair sparkled in the sunlight.

"Glad I found you. Your mom said you'd come this way. Hi, Taylor," Tabitha added before narrowing her eyes at the puppy, her voice not much more than a growl. "Rita."

The dog answered by nuzzling her black boot.

"She likes you," Taylor said.

"*Hmmmmph*. She likes my taste in shoes." Tabitha grimaced as she carefully moved her foot away from the small dog. "Did you know puppies can cause two thousand dollars of damage to a house?"

"Please don't tell my mom that," Midnight said. "She's already freaking out at how much it costs to set up a café. Apparently silverware is more expensive than gold these days."

"I tell you, finger food's the way to go," Tabitha said, and Midnight giggled.

"How was your date last night?"

Tabitha shook her head and sighed. "He had to cancel at the last minute. He had to see his grandma again."

"Are you okay?" Midnight swallowed. She hated that Tyson kept canceling on her friend. What was he up to? Then again, girls in glass houses shouldn't throw stones. Especially when they broke dates to go to the swimming pool because they had to chase phantom ringmasters instead. Or stood someone up to work in their mom's café.

Was she really any different than Tyson?

She made a mental note to make it up to Logan.

"Sure." Tabitha shrugged before staring Rita down. "How far are you walking?"

"To the park and back," Midnight explained before realizing that Tabitha's eyes were gleaming. *She has news.* "What's going on? Have you found something?"

"No, but Logan has. I went to see him before coming to your place but he wasn't there, so I called him. He said to meet him at Cookies and Cakes."

"He wants cake at ten in the morning?" Midnight lifted an eyebrow. Not that she was complaining. "Did he say why?"

Tabitha shook her head. "He was strangely mysterious. Usually I can crack him like an egg. Hopefully, he learned something at the hospital yesterday. We could use a break."

"Go do your Ghostbuster stuff," Taylor cut in. "I have music. I have headphones. I have coffee."

Midnight opened her mouth to ask if she was sure, but Taylor just shrugged and headed in the other direction, the little puppy bouncing along beside her.

"I'm still having difficulty adjusting to the Taylor reboot," Tabitha said as they headed to the bus stop.

"You're not the only one." Midnight still felt guilty she hadn't been able to stop her sister from seeing first-hand what planodiume could do to a person. "Mom's freaking out because Taylor hardly leaves the house. Last night she even offered to buy concert tickets for Twenty One Pilots, and Taylor turned them down."

"I didn't realize she was still so messed up by what had happened."

"You're not the only one," Midnight said as a bus pulled up and they climbed on to make the short trip to Cookies and Cakes.

* * *

Logan was already sitting at their favorite table, look-ing all kinds of cute with a plain T-shirt against his olive-brown skin. Next to him was a girl with ebony hair

and a heart-shaped face. Her large, black eyes were lumi-
nous, and she had a bandage on her arm.

"Who's that?" Midnight asked, not quite sure what to
make of the fact Logan was sitting with a pretty girl. At
what was meant to be *their* table.

"I have no idea," Tabitha muttered as Logan waved
them over.

He grinned, though his attention still seemed to be on
the girl next to him. "This is Akari. We were together at
soccer camp a couple of years ago."

Soccer camp? Logan liked soccer? Midnight's confusion increased.

"Hello." Tabitha gave the girl a cool nod and sat down.

"Hi." Midnight followed suit.

"So nice to meet you both." Akari gave them a shy
smile and fiddled with the frayed edge of her bandage.
"Messi's been telling me all about you."

"Messi?" Midnight pushed her glasses farther up her
nose as if that would somehow help her understand what
was going on. It didn't.

"It's nothing." He flushed. "Just a silly nickname."

"Silly? Are you serious? At soccer camp we were playing

a game, and Messi—I mean, Logan—scored the most amazing goal," Akari explained. "It was crazy. The coach still talks about it. So we named him after Lionel Messi."

Midnight blinked. She wasn't sure who Lionel Messi was, but it seemed like a big deal.

"So you guys haven't seen each other in a while?" Tabitha asked, her voice cool.

"Not since camp, but we bumped into each other yesterday at the hospital," Logan said. "She was on the Amazing House of Horrors Ghost Ride."

Suddenly Midnight understood. *Akari* was a clue.

"And I was trying not to cry like a baby," Akari held up her arm and pulled a face. "Still can't believe Messi managed to catch me at my worst."

"If I'd sprained my arm, I would've cried too." Logan gave her a warm smile.

"We heard about the accident. You must've been scared silly," Tabitha said, appearing to relax.

"I'm not going to lie. It was horrible." Akari wrinkled her nose, which made her look cuter than ever. Midnight tried not to be jealous.

"Do you remember what happened?" she asked.

"That's the crazy thing. I'm not even sure. One minute I was screaming as the train went through a really scary section with loads of skeletons and cobwebs hanging everywhere, then everything went blank and my arm was hurting. The operators felt so bad. They said there'd never been an accident on the train before."

Midnight, Tabitha, and Logan exchanged looks. It wasn't the first time they'd heard that.

"She's sprained her arm, but the doctor said she was lucky not to have broken it." Logan's face was marred with concern.

"It wasn't so bad." Akari lowered her gaze. "It definitely helped that you kept me company at the hospital until my mom arrived."

"Anyone would've done the same," he mumbled, color rising in his cheeks.

"Well, it was nice," she said. "Though you have to ignore all the weird things I was saying. I think it was the shock."

"What weird things?" Tabitha immediately asked.

Akari gave Logan a nervous glance, as if unsure if she should say anything. He nodded, and she sighed.

"Okay, but please remember that it was dark and creepy and my arm really hurt. But before they turned on the lights and called the ambulance, I was sure that I saw a man staring at me."

Midnight caught her breath. "Did you see what he looked like? What was he wearing?" She remembered the scrap of gold rope they'd found. *Had it come from someone's clothing?*

Akari shook her head. "It's all a blur. I don't remember his clothes. I'm sorry."

"It's okay," Logan quickly assured her.

"Thanks." Akari gave him a shy smile, just as her phone beeped. She scanned the screen. "That's my mom. She's waiting in the parking lot to take me for another appointment."

"Sure. So, I guess I'll see you around," Logan said as he stood up.

"Definitely," Akari agreed before giving Midnight and Tabitha a smile. "It was really nice to meet you both."

Tabitha leaned forward as soon as Akari had walked out of the café. "Well, that was a stroke of luck."

"A stroke of luck she almost broke her arm?" Logan's mouth tightened into a flat line.

"That's not what I meant," Tabitha protested. "Of course it's bad she got hurt. But it's good for us that you know her."

"Sorry." Logan ran a hand through his head. "It shook me up seeing her at the hospital. But I did get a reading. Here," he said as he retrieved his Ping.

SED: 15.02%

Life-Span Depletion: 2.4 years

Midnight let out a gasp. Akari was their age, yet she'd lost almost two and a half years of her life. Not to mention sprained her arm. No wonder Logan was upset.

"Poor Akari." Tabitha's face went pale.

"We'll get it back for her," Logan said fiercely. "And for everyone else. I managed to check on the others who were injured. They'd each lost the same amount."

"This is getting worse," Midnight said as Logan's phone beeped. He studied the screen and then looked up, his eyes wide.

"Everything okay?" Tabitha said. "Because I'm not sure we can take any more bad news."

"Actually," he said slowly, his voice almost dazed, "I think this is good news. It's a text from Akari. She just remembered something else." He held up the screen for them all to see.

Messi. I'm such a dope. The weird guy I saw? I swear he was on crutches like he had a broken leg.

The three friends stared at each other, none of them speaking. They didn't need to because they already knew someone who had a broken leg.

Joseph.

Joseph the clown.

"How's that even possible? He was a victim of one of the accidents." Midnight finally found her voice.

"Or was he?" Tabitha's eyebrow shot up. "Isn't it possible he staged his own accident?"

"But why put himself through it?" Logan asked.

"Because if he knows about planodiume," Midnight said, "maybe he also knows about Black Streams and the Agency of Spectral Protection. He wanted to make sure he had an alibi in case anyone at ASP figured out what he was doing." Adrenaline flared through her as it all came together.

Logan nodded. "And it makes sense because Tabitha told me you saw Joseph when you were searching for clues yesterday. Which puts him at the scene of the crime."

"Plus, check this out." Tabitha had been tapping away on her phone, searching the Internet, but she stopped and held up her screen. "In the last five years, the circus has visited eight towns that are Black Streams, and each time Joseph was injured on the first night."

"So he lied about there being no accidents, and he's purposely done things to take suspicion away from him," Logan surmised. "He's been with the circus long enough to have been able to find Eduardo De Rossi's journal."

Something nagged at the back of Midnight's mind at the mention of the journal. Then she stiffened.

The journal…was a book! And where had she just seen books? She turned to her friends and grinned.

"Guess what Joseph has in his trailer?" she said. "A whole shelf of books. It did seem weird because he told us at the hospital he hated reading, but I didn't think too much about it. If Akari's right about seeing Joseph at the Amazing House of Horrors Ghost Ride, then the journal could very well be in the bookshelf."

"Exactly." Tabitha grinned as they got to their feet. "We finally know what we need to do."

Midnight nodded.

They had to get back into Joseph's trailer. If Eduardo De Rossi's journal was there, they'd know once for all who they were up against. And hopefully that would lead them to the relic and the disappearing tent.

They had to get that journal.

CHAPTER THIRTEEN

"No," Ryan said.

"I don't understand." Midnight stared at her supervisor. "Wouldn't it be nice if we left another bunch of flowers?" She thrust forward the wilted daisies she'd bought from the corner store on the way to the bus stop. She hadn't even minded the strange looks her green coveralls had attracted from the clerk.

She was so close to finding Eduardo de Rossi's journal and figuring out what the relic was.

Ryan shrugged, his expression unmoved. "We only did that because Carlo told me to. If you want to take it up with the ringmaster, be my guest. But, for the record, if you do, you're fired."

Without the master key to Joseph's trailer, there was no way they could look for the journal there.

"It's no big deal," Tabitha cut in, her voice cool. "We were just trying to do you a favor."

"What do you mean?" Ryan's giraffe-neck stretched forward. "How's this a favor?"

Tabitha frowned, as if debating whether she should say anything. "I heard Carlo was really impressed at how much effort the cleanup crew went to for Joseph when he came out of hospital. But I guess he won't expect you to do the same thing again."

"Did he tell you that?" Ryan's face paled.

"I really can't say." Tabitha crossed her fingers behind her back.

"Right." Ryan coughed and fumbled for the master keys. "Now that I think of it, leaving Joseph some more flowers is a great idea. Can you do it right now?"

"Sure." Tabitha gave an indifferent shrug and reached for the keys.

The three friends didn't speak until they were out

of earshot.

"Tab, that was amazing. I see an Oscar in your future." Midnight grinned.

"I have my moments." Tabitha shrugged as they hurried to Joseph's trailer.

News of the accident at the Amazing House of Horrors Ghost Ride had gotten out, and the crowds had thinned in response, but that didn't reassure Midnight. Until they could prove who was responsible, no one was safe.

There was no sign of the clown when they reached the trailer.

The plan was for Tabitha and Logan to stand guard while Midnight went in to search for the journal. Even if it was there, she couldn't risk taking it. She'd have to photograph every page. Thank goodness ASP had provided her with a phone that had enough storage to hold her spreadsheets, her music, *and* a book designed to bring someone back from the dead.

She twisted the key into the lock and turned the handle, her heart pounding. *Relax.* If Joseph came, her friends would keep him distracted.

The trailer was much as she'd left it, apart from a clown suit hanging from the ceiling. Without a person inside, it made for an eerie silhouette.

The flowers from the other day were still in the vase, but Midnight went straight to the bookshelf. It was deeper than she'd first suspected, and she carefully lifted away the collection of paperbacks. A soft gasp escaped her lips.

There at the back was an old leather book.

It was icy cold against her fingers as she flipped up the cover and studied the inscription.

If you're reading this book, I am dead.

But with your help, I won't be for long…

So it was true. Eduardo had written a journal about how to bring himself back to life, and Joseph was the person doing it.

It was one thing to have a theory, but another to have hard evidence.

Midnight's hands shook as she sent her friends a text.

It's here. I've found it.

She held up her phone and took a photograph before turning the page.

* * *

"Rise and shine," her mom said, accompanied by the pitter-patter of little puppy feet running across the wooden floorboards of Midnight's bedroom. Midnight groaned and rubbed her eyes.

Was it morning already?

She'd been up for most of the night reading through the printout of Eduardo De Rossi's journal.

It was filled with extensive details of how he'd discovered planodiume while working in a European circus. One of the trapeze artists had taught him how to steal it, and Eduardo had carried the knowledge back to Berry.

At first he'd only taken small amounts, but as his performances had improved, he'd increased the levels he was stealing.

18th May 1898: It is extraordinary. The animals now recognize me as their leader and will perform however I wish. My power has grown so strong that soon the world will see me for the master I am. However, I do need to be more careful about how much energy I take. Another woman died last week. Thankfully, she was old, and the fools put it down to a heart condition. I must not take any more energy until we go on tour.

20th September 1898: One of the elephants was doing poorly, and by evening the vet pronounced her dead. I decided to see if I could bring her back using the energy I'd collected. It worked, and while the ignorant folks around me called it a miracle, I knew the truth. It was no miracle; it's because I have the ultimate power.

15th May 1899: I have a plan. Why only use these immense powers in this lifetime? I am taking steps to ensure that no matter what happens, I can be brought back from death. To do so, I need a relic. I have experimented with several items, but none have proved satisfactory. Until now.

That entry was written the day before Eduardo had been killed by the angry mob. More chilling was the note scrawled in the margin. The handwriting and ink were different, and Midnight bet her favorite sneakers that it belonged to Joseph.

I've figured it out. I know what the relic is.

"Morning." Midnight pried her eyes open in time to see Rita making her way under the bed, dragging the leash.

She scrambled to her feet so quickly that her head spun as she scooped up the puppy. Not only were there numerous weapons under there, but it was where she'd stashed the journal page printouts. Knowing Rita, she'd eat them.

"I made you breakfast." Her mom beamed, holding a tray in her hands. It smelled of buckwheat pancakes, berries, and honey. Midnight's nose twitched, but her stomach sank. Food bribes could only mean one thing.

"What's Taylor done now?" She put Rita on the bed and took the tray.

Her mom picked up the little black-and-white puppy and sat down next to her. "Nothing…which is the problem. I was supposed to go with Phil to pick up the tables and chairs for the café, but I still haven't found a hostess and have to do more interviews."

Midnight had been in the process of spearing a berry, but she put down her fork. "What are you saying?"

"I know you're busy with your new job, but Phil needs help loading the van, and Taylor's refusing to go."

Midnight closed her eyes. It was her day off from the circus, but she'd planned to meet her friends so they could follow Joseph and find the tent. To put an end to the spectral energy thefts before anyone else could get hurt.

But if she said no, her mom would probably get even more annoyed with Taylor, and Midnight still felt guilty about what her sister was going through.

"Okay. What time's he going?"

"Just as soon as you've had breakfast and a shower." Her mom's face broke into a smile as she stood up. "Thank you, honey. I really appreciate it. And cross your fingers that I find someone for the hostess job."

"All crossed." She held up her hand. She liked helping her mom and new stepdad, but it was hard when there was so much on the line.

* * *

"How's the job going?" Phil asked as he drove along Fir Tree Avenue.

He wasn't dressed in Viking gear, but there was some chain mail in the backseat and a notebook filled with runic writing on the dashboard. Midnight knew it was his to-do list for the upcoming summer solstice party he was organizing. At one time Midnight would've found this stuff odd, but now she thought it was kind of cool.

"It's fun," she said, crossing her fingers. "Though my boss is obsessed with litter. He gets really mad when you miss picking up a hot dog wrapper."

"My first boss was a bit like that." Phil stopped at a set of lights. "I worked at a car dealership washing all the cars. He hated when anyone messed up the wax."

"Sounds like he and Ryan have a lot in common." Midnight glanced out the window, only to see a familiar black hoodie.

Tyson?

She pressed her nose closer to the glass as a flash of long, blond hair poked out from under the hood. It was definitely him. He scanned the street before walking purposefully toward a blue Toyota.

Midnight caught her breath, but before she could

see what happened next, the lights changed and Phil hit the accelerator.

She craned her head. Tyson was talking to someone else. Who was it? Nerves danced in her stomach, and she laced her fingers together.

"Everything okay?" Phil asked, glancing at her hands.

Apart from the fact my best friend's boyfriend is acting shady?

"It's fine." She swallowed before turning to him. "What were you saying about the car thefts the other day?"

"Oh." He let out a pained sigh. "It's still happening. Cars aren't being stolen. Someone's just breaking into them. And half the time they don't even take anything. It's almost like it's for a dare. Though the damage they're causing is anything but funny."

"Do the police have any idea who's behind it?" She tried not to fidget. Phil shook his head as they pulled into the store parking lot.

"No, though I suspect it's bored teenagers. Crazy, right?"

"Yeah, crazy." Midnight gulped and climbed out of the car, still unsure whether she should say anything to

Tabitha, especially if she didn't have proof. Before she could decide, her phone beeped.

It was Tabitha.

Meet me at the cemetery. I know what the relic is.

CHAPTER FOURTEEN

"I got here as fast as I could." Midnight puffed as she reached Berry Cemetery. It was surrounded by a huge wrought-iron fence, and the entrance was flanked by giant oak trees.

"It's okay," Tabitha said. "And sorry for the secrecy, but I wanted to show you myself."

"Where's Logan?" Midnight turned around.

"Oh." Tabitha winced. "I was hoping you wouldn't ask that."

"What do you mean?"

"Don't get mad. And whatever you do, *don't* read anything into it."

"Into what? Tabitha, what's going on?"

"He was with me doing research. He was mind-mapping ideas about how the purple tent could possibly stay hidden when he got a call from Akari."

Midnight's mouth went dry. "Oh."

"She'd bumped into a friend from soccer camp and made plans for them all to meet up," Tabitha said in a hurry. "I swear he didn't want to go. He tried to say no about three times, but I think he felt bad for her."

"Right." Midnight remembered to shut her mouth. It made sense. Logan was always considerate and kind. Of course he wouldn't want to hurt Akari's feelings.

"It's no big deal," Tabitha said. "He really likes you, Midnight. Please don't freak out."

"I'm not," she lied, and forced a smile onto her face.

It was bad enough that Akari was cute *and* seemed to know Logan better than Midnight did. Even worse, she was free to do what she wanted.

To hang out with friends.

To laugh.

To be a regular twelve-year-old.

Why *wouldn't* Logan like her?

If Midnight had been alone, she would've written everything out in a neat spreadsheet. A pros-and-cons list so she could get clarity and figure out what was going with Logan and Akari. And if she should be worried. Instead, she was stuck with thoughts all jumbled in her head.

Not to mention that she didn't have time to worry about it.

"I'm okay. I promise," Midnight told her friend. "So, what's this big clue you've found?"

"I'd rather show you." Tabitha pushed open the wrought-iron gate.

They walked past the large mausoleums to the older part of the cemetery. The grass was mown, but many of the headstones were broken and crumbling. Midnight followed her friend, whose long, black skirt swished in the light breeze.

"Here we are." Tabitha stopped in front of an obelisk headstone. It was over six foot tall and a dull-gray color. The point speared into the sky and had a granite snake wrapped around it, its scales carved in a pattern like frayed rope.

Farther down the headstone were three names, all carved in gold.

Carmen De Rossi
Beloved Mother, Sister, Wife
Born April 5th 1836, Died June 13th 1886

It was Eduardo's mother. The name below was his father's, the two names separated by a golden pair of wedding rings that had been carved into the granite. They were held together by a golden coil.

Antonio De Rossi
Loving Husband, Father, and Son
Born June 1st 1825, Died September 12th 1888

And underneath them both was their son.

Eduardo De Rossi
Dearest Husband and Father
Born October 8th 1856, Died July 10th 1899

"Look," Tabitha said, pointing to the golden wedding rings that had been carved between Antonio's and Carmen's names. "I think these are a clue."

"All I see is the snake." Midnight frowned.

"It's hard not to," Tabitha agreed. "But remember how we figured out that Joseph had mentioned a snake to mislead us? To make us suspect Zelda instead?" She motioned to the rings again. "This makes so much more sense. We know Eduardo was very close to his father and wanted to make the circus a success in his memory."

Midnight gasped. "I just thought of something! When we saw Joseph behind the ghost ride, he had on lots of gold jewelry. I just thought he had strange taste. Do you think the relic is Antonio's wedding ring?"

Tabitha nodded. "I do. We don't know how Joseph found the journal, but let's assume he stole it from Carlo. If that's the case, Joseph could've just as easily stolen other personal possessions. Like the wedding rings that belonged to Eduardo's parents."

"So, now we have to find the tent and wait for Joseph to go in. Then I can use Rockstar to destroy the relic." When Midnight said that out loud, it almost sounded easy to do.

"The sooner the better," Tabitha agreed. "But right now it's just the three of us, and it's taking too long to search the circus. I was thinking we could tell Tyson about the ASP and our real job. He could help us find Joseph. Many hands make light work."

Oh. Midnight sucked in a breath. After their last case, where she'd broken Agency rules and told Logan what they were doing, she and Tabitha had been given permission to use their own judgment about who they shared their secret with. Plus, Tyson wasn't just Tabitha's boyfriend; he was also Logan's best friend.

"I know you're worried about what he might say, but I swear he isn't like that," Tabitha said. "He already thinks you're cool. And remember when you told Logan? He was impressed, and you'd been scared about nothing… So, what do you think?"

Midnight swallowed. Logan, Tabitha, and even Taylor hadn't judged her when they'd learned about her special ability, but it was still daunting for someone else to know. Especially someone who she'd caught in a lie.

Part of her longed to tell Tabitha *why* she was worried, but the other part of her didn't want to upset her friend.

Especially not without proof.

"Can I think about it?"

"Of course." Tabitha nodded, though there was a hint of disappointment in her eyes. "Maybe it won't even matter. Hopefully, we'll find Joseph before he can hurt anyone else."

* * *

"How's it possible to lose someone on crutches?" Tabitha complained the following afternoon as they emptied their last bag of trash. The day was hot and cloudless, and the sickly sweet scent of cotton candy filled the air.

Despite the most recent accident, long lines of people were waiting for the rides. Midnight wanted to warn them to be careful, but of course she couldn't do that without telling them why.

Thankfully, Tabitha hadn't been upset about their conversation yesterday and hadn't brought up Tyson's name again. That was a relief.

"What if Joseph's already in the tent?" Midnight wiped the sweat from her brow, trying to mask her panic. They'd spent the last four hours searching for the clown, but there was no sign of him, and everyone had given them the same dazed answer: *I'm sure he's somewhere.*

"If he is, he can't stay in there all day," Logan pointed out. "We'll just need to keep looking. For Joseph *and* the tent."

"I have an idea," Tabitha announced. "Midnight, I think you should talk to Zelda again."

"Do you think she'll tell us anything helpful?" Logan frowned. "If Joseph's using planodiume to wipe everyone's minds, she might not."

"But we're running out of time," Tabitha replied. "And it seemed like she was trying to warn Midnight."

"True." Logan flipped open his notebook and nodded. "Here it is. She said, 'If you're smart, you'll not see it either.'"

Midnight shivered. Zelda had also said: *You're not special.*

"I still can't figure out what that means—'you'll *not* see it.'" Logan rubbed his chin. "Because if Midnight *can't* see something, what good is that? Unless there's a hidden meaning. We might as well follow up."

"What do you say?" Tabitha turned to Midnight, blue eyes concerned.

It's a bad idea. The worst.

It was also all they had.

"I guess it doesn't hurt," Midnight said.

It didn't take long to reach Zelda's tent. The fortune-teller was sitting under the awning, absently toying with the fringe of her scarf. Long shadows fell across her face, and Midnight suppressed a gasp.

Streaks of gray ran through Zelda's formerly ebony hair, while a network of wrinkles covered her face, and her hands were curled into arthritic claws. She looked about eighty years old.

Peter Gallagher was right. Joseph had obviously stopped trying to be careful about stealing spectral energy from people. He knew his time was running out.

"You shouldn't be here," Zelda said, her voice sharp.

"Please," Midnight said. "I need to talk to you. I have money."

Zelda pursed her lips together and tilted her head before slowly rising to her feet. "I don't want your money, girl. And it's too dangerous out here. Come inside."

"Thank you."

Zelda shuffled through to the tent. Midnight followed

her and suppressed a gasp. Even the interior of the tent had changed, as if the life had been sucked out of it. Gone were the rich burgundy and gold that'd been threaded through the rugs and veils, replaced with dull, muted shades of beige and gray.

"You can't stay long. It's not safe."

"That's why I need your help," Midnight said. "We know Joseph's responsible for what's happening to you and the others, and I have a way to stop him. Please, you have to tell me where he is."

Zelda's mouth opened, as if she wanted to speak, but no sound came out. Her hands clenched, and she shut her eyes. She was clearly trying to fight the mind control. Despite all Zelda's efforts, it seemed too strong.

"I'm sorry." Zelda lowered herself into the chair, her face pale from the exertion. "Please. Save us."

Midnight nodded. "I promise I'll find a way to get your stolen time back."

She walked out into the daylight where Logan was waiting, looking concerned. Midnight wasn't the only one shocked by Zelda's appearance.

"Anything?" he asked.

"No. She tried to tell me something, but the words wouldn't come out. Where's Tabitha?"

"She's gone to check on Carlo. I said we'd meet at the big top."

"I didn't even think about Carlo," Midnight said, rubbing her arms as they walked through the crowd. All around them, people looked gray and drained. Was this Joseph's doing?

"I didn't think about him either. I feel bad that I couldn't finish my research yesterday," Logan suddenly said. "Did Tabitha tell you about Akari?"

"Sort of," Midnight mumbled, her cheeks heating up. "It's no big deal."

"Sure. I just didn't—"

He was cut off by a piercing howl as a streak of golden light split down through the summer sky like a thunderbolt.

The hairs on the back of Midnight's neck stiffened, and a noise screamed in her ear, like a thousand bees filled with rage. Her knees buckled.

Spectral transference. It was happening again.

"What's going on?" Logan's voice dragged her from

her trance. Midnight blinked and began to run in the direction of the raging golden energy.

"It's back. Somewhere over here."

"The carousel," Logan said as they broke through the crowd and came to a horrified halt.

The carousel was a magnificent old-fashioned ride with richly painted horses and hundreds of tiny lights covering the bronze-colored ceiling. But now golden light swirled around the carousel, turning it faster and faster. Supernatural metallic sparks shot out as the tinkling music rose into a high-pitched cacophony. Riders were clinging to the necks of the horses as a piercing scream rent the air.

"Somebody stop it!" a bystander cried, but the carousel continued to spin, the air around it swooshing and swirling in response.

Midnight searched the crowd for Joseph. He had to be here somewhere. Controlling it. Stealing the energy. Her fingers itched to drag out Rockstar and fix what was happening, but that wouldn't work. She *had* to find Joseph.

She scanned the area, but there was no sign of him. She ran, searching around the nearby tents. *Where is he?*

A shattering screech filled the air, and the brilliant golden light was gone. The carousel came to a juddering halt, and the terrified screams jabbed at Midnight's ears. Sirens rang through the air, and a fire engine drove up, splitting apart the crowds. Tabitha's father climbed out of the truck and took charge, barking directions to his colleagues.

An ambulance squealed to a halt and raced to treat the injured, while huddles of people held up their phones, taking pictures and speaking in horrified whispers.

Midnight pushed through the crowd in time to see a frantic mother clamber up to the carousel and lift her terrified son from his horse, unclutching his grip.

The boy's soft blond hair was damp with sweat, and a smear of ice cream was on his T-shirt...*and his eyes were golden*.

Midnight turned to see an old woman who was being helped into the ambulance. She had the same blank expression and glittering golden eyes.

Dread caught in Midnight's throat. Everyone on the carousel had been affected.

Tabitha pushed through the crowd, clutching at her Ping.

"Are you all right?" her friend panted.

"I couldn't stop it." Midnight shook her head. All these people were hurt because she couldn't do anything. Then she noticed Tabitha's haunted eyes. "What are the life-span readings?"

"Not good. This was for a guy who looked about thirty years old," Tabitha's voice was little above a whisper as she held up her device so Midnight could see the screen.

SED: 40%

Life-Span Depletion: 15 years

Someone had lost fifteen years of their life. Peter Gallagher had said that when SED levels went over fifty percent, the situation became really serious. More and more energy was being stolen from people.

Never had Midnight felt so helpless.

CHAPTER FIFTEEN

"Feeling better?" her mom asked the following morning when Midnight walked into the kitchen. The counters were filled with metal goblets and heavy wooden plates for the solstice party.

Midnight rubbed her eyes and tried not to yawn. News of the carousel accident had traveled quickly, and she hadn't felt up to talking about it, so she'd gone to bed early, saying she felt sick.

It wasn't a lie. The white faces and terrified screams of everyone caught on the ride had swirled around in her head all night, until her temples pounded and her eyelids went heavy.

"A little." She headed to the pantry in search of food.

"Good." Her mom folded away the local paper she'd been reading and stood up. "Perhaps it's for the best the circus is closing early."

"What?" Midnight spun back around so fast that the plastic jar of peanut butter fell to the floor and rolled away. "It's still here for another three days."

Three days left for me to stop Joseph.

"You didn't know?" her mom said in surprise as she held up the newspaper. "It says here that due to the numerous accidents at Cirque Fantastic, the fire chief decided the show can't go on. The last performance will be tonight, and they pack up and leave tomorrow.

Only one day left?

Just then Rita raced into the kitchen and headed straight to Phil's old slipper. The little puppy had claimed it as her own, and it now looked more like an explosion of wool rather than something that went on a foot.

Taylor followed a moment later. "What's going on?" she asked, raising an eyebrow.

"I was telling Midnight the circus is closing tonight,"

their mom said. She walked over to the door just as the sound of Phil's car pulling into the driveway could be heard. "That's my cue. We're off to interview staff. Can one of you please wash the dishes?"

"Sure," Taylor said, as their mom gathered up her giant tote bag. Once she was gone, Taylor hissed. "This is the last day? Please tell me you're getting closer to solving this thing!"

"We're trying," Midnight said. "We know Joseph's responsible *and* that to stop him we need to destroy the gold wedding ring on his finger. It once belonged to Eduardo's father. But first we have to find him. There's a good chance he's hiding out in an invisible tent," she said, trying to force down her panic. But something Tabitha had said came back to her. *Many hands make light work.* Tabitha was right. Midnight turned to her sister. "We could use some help. Having an extra person could make all the difference."

Taylor stood still as her face drained of color. "I-I'm not sure I can do that. Plus, what about Rita?"

At the mention of her name, the little puppy reappeared from the pantry, where she'd been playing with the plastic peanut butter jar. She came skidding to a halt, pink tongue darting in and out of her mouth. Then she gave another bark and ran over to where her leash was lying on the floor. She barked again and pawed it, urging Taylor to pick it up.

"I wouldn't ask for help if we weren't desperate," Midnight said. She noticed how her sister's hands were shaking as she knelt and patted the puppy. "Forget I asked. We'll find Joseph today and stop him. I promise."

Taylor let out a long breath and nodded as she clipped the leash onto Rita's collar. "I'm sorry. It's not that I don't want to—"

"It's okay," Midnight said.

Tabitha and Logan appeared at the back door, their faces grim. They were as worried as she was. Midnight plastered on a smile and said goodbye to her sister. Of course they would figure it out. They didn't have a choice.

* * *

They had been searching the circus for three hours, but there was no sign of Joseph or the tent.

"Did you try looking in the fourth quadrant?" Midnight asked.

"Twice. And in all the other quadrants," Tabitha replied as she dropped her trash bag and shook her head. "I should call Tyson for help. I know you wanted to think about it, but we're running out of time."

Midnight's head throbbed. She didn't want to hurt her friend's feelings, but it was so hard to say yes, especially when she'd twice seen Tyson acting shady. If he was lying to Tabitha, how could she trust him? But if she didn't trust him, then Tabitha would be hurt.

Or worse…hundreds of people would never have their stolen time returned.

"I think we should wait a little bit longer."

"Longer?" Tabitha glanced at the lowering sun. "By the end of the night the whole place will be shut down. We need to make a decision."

"I know." Midnight rolled her shoulders. "I want to. It's just that—"

"Just what?" Tabitha came to a halt and folded her arms. "Do you have something against Tyson?"

Midnight opened her mouth, but the words caught in her throat.

"Forget it." Tabitha cut her off with a shake of her

black hair. "I'm going to double-check the big top. Unless you don't trust me."

"Of course I trust you—" Midnight started to say but before she could finish, her friend had stomped away, passing Logan as he approached holding his notebook.

"What just happened?"

"Nothing." Midnight shook her head. Tyson was also Logan's best friend, and again, she didn't want to say anything without proof. But she also hated lying. She sighed. "Tabitha wants to ask Tyson to help us."

"Is that such a bad idea? The circus closes down tonight, and by tomorrow they'll be pulling out of town. If Joseph brings Eduardo back—"

"I know," Midnight cut in. "It'll be too late."

"So, what's the problem? I've been friends with Tyson since we were six years old. Midnight, he'd never betray your secret."

She let out a soft sigh as they walked to the carousel. "The other day when he was meant to be at his grandmother's house, I saw him at Dingle Donuts just as a car was broken into. He was acting shifty."

Logan frowned. "His grandmother does live near Dingle

Donuts. He might've been running errands for her."

"I guess." Midnight nodded. "Then I saw him later lurking around the cars in a parking lot. It seemed odd, but I know how bad it is to jump to conclusions. I've really messed up. Tabitha's never going to talk to me again."

"Yes, she will. You just need to tell her what you've told me. She understands how scary it is for you to share your secret."

"I hope so."

"I *know* so," Logan corrected as he took his phone out of his pocket. "Let's call her."

"Okay." Midnight nodded.

"No answer. I'll send a text," he said. Midnight caught her breath, waiting to see if Tabitha would respond right away. There was no reply. "Try not to freak out. You know Tabitha doesn't hold grudges."

"I know," Midnight said, trying to sound positive.

As they squeezed their way past a crowd of people lined up for the Ferris wheel, a familiar voice drifted over. It was Akari, who was kneeling on the ground, pleading with a young boy who looked about seven or eight.

"Kiro, come on. We need to go home," she said. At

the sight of Midnight and Logan, she scrambled up, gripping the young boy's hand in hers. She was dressed in a black swing skirt and bright-pink sneakers that matched the bandage on her arm. "H-hey, you guys."

"Everything okay?" Logan asked.

"Not really." She shook her head. "Kiro wanted one more go on the rides before the circus closes, and he bugged me into bringing him. Except now he wants to go on the Ferris wheel. But, after what happened—"

"You're just a chicken," Kiro said, his lower lip poking out in a mulish expression. "I want to go on it."

"And *I* want to go home," Akari said, her eyes pleading. "Please, Kiro."

"No." The little boy stomped the ground. Logan was quiet as he looked from Akari to Kiro. Then he lowered himself so he was at eye level with the little boy.

"How about I go on the ride with you?"

"Really?" Kiro caught his breath.

"Really," Logan agreed, and Kiro danced in delight.

"Messi, thank you," Akari said, her eyes glittering. "I never should've come back here. I didn't realize how scared it'd make me feel."

"It's fine," he said before turning to Midnight. "Sorry. I hope you don't mind."

She grimaced.

She knew it was the right thing for him to do. After all, the sooner the little boy had his ride, the sooner Akari could get him to safety. But part of her was mad. Logan was meant to be helping her. Meant to be *her* boyfriend. She swallowed it down and gave a curt nod.

"Why should I mind?" she said and winced as a flash of hurt spread across Logan's face. He opened his mouth as if he wanted to speak, but before he could, Kiro tugged at his arm.

"Come on." The small boy began to drag Logan and Akari toward the Ferris wheel. A lump formed in Midnight's throat as they disappeared into the crowd without bothering to even look back.

Tears prickled in the corner of her eyes, but she brushed them away. It was stupid to be jealous, but she couldn't help it. Even worse, she couldn't talk to Tabitha because her best friend was mad at her. Everything was falling apart.

No. She caught herself.

She was just overreacting. To Logan and Akari, and to Tabitha's request for Tyson to join them. She couldn't fix things with Logan until after he got off the ride, but she could definitely say "sorry" to Tabitha.

Feeling better, she turned toward the big top. The sooner she—

"Sav, that's so gross. You'd better delete it or else. My neck looks freaky."

Midnight stopped just feet from where Sav and Lucy were examining a photograph, both with their lips pursed in concentration.

"It doesn't look nearly as freaky as my pinkie finger." Sav gave a delicate wrinkle of her nose, and Midnight blinked.

Who cares how their pinkie finger looks in a selfie?

Wait. Don't answer that.

Luckily, the two girls were so absorbed that they didn't notice Midnight had almost walked into them. Thank goodness. Her day had been lousy enough without getting teased by her ex-friends.

She ducked into a small gap between two nearby tents and pressed herself farther into the shadow of the awning. Finally happy with the shot, the two girls sauntered in her direction. Midnight stiffened and willed herself to be invisible.

Please don't see me. Please don't see me.

Sav stopped several feet away from where Midnight was hunched and checked her lip gloss in the mirror app on her phone. Midnight held her breath, not daring to move until the two girls finally disappeared into the crowd.

That'd been way too close.

She stepped back out, and a flicker of smudgy purple caught in the corner of her eye. She slowly turned around to look at the tent she'd just been hiding next to.

It was the tent. She'd found it.

Inadvertently helped by Sav and Lucy.

Relief filled her as she called Tabitha. There was still no answer, so she quickly sent another text, as well as one to Logan. No matter what was going on with her friends, they needed to know that she'd found the tent.

She unzipped her backpack and lifted Rockstar out. The strange weapon seemed too light. Too delicate to work. Hopefully she'd be proved wrong. She flipped on the switches, and it hummed to life. Then she slung the strap over her shoulder and wrapped her hand around the nozzle.

Either Joseph was already in there, or she would wait until he turned up.

And then it would be over.

She reached into her pocket for the button-sized tracking device and pressed it into the canvas of the tent. It emitted two sharp beeps, then seemed to disappear so it couldn't be detected. At least now her friends could find her.

She tightened her grip on Rockstar and stepped inside.

Darkness swallowed her as she walked down the long corridor until she reached the domed center.

The giant posters began to ripple, as if the figures trapped inside them were about to step out into the world. The floor-to-ceiling shelves were filled with masks, wigs, and jars of strange specimens that glittered and gleamed. The old megaphone seemed to have grown, and the golden whip undulated as if it was alive, while the empty cages, giant mirrors, and unused carnival rides all seemed to mock her as she walked past.

Midnight ignored them as she moved to the center of the room where the coffin-shaped box lay. The tasseled purple cloth that had covered it was crumpled on the floor, and floating above it was the body of Eduardo De Rossi.

His silhouette glimmered in a golden light—except for eight black pieces dotted around his frame like missing pieces of a jigsaw puzzle.

Like they were waiting to be filled in with stolen spectral energy.

And when it was done, he'd once again be human.

Midnight's stomach twisted in a sickening knot.

All the people who'd been hurt in the last few days had given years of their future to bring Eduardo De Rossi back to life. Time they might never get back. She fumbled for her phone and sent her friends another text.

Why hadn't they come?

Because they're still mad at me.

"Well, look who it is…" a familiar voice said, and Midnight slowly turned. Joseph was leaning forward on his crutches. He was wearing his clown costume, complete with blue hair and a grotesque smile, but all the jewelry he'd been wearing earlier was gone. All but a single gleaming golden ring on his finger.

She hadn't noticed it before. It had been hidden by the other garish jewelry he'd been wearing. Hidden in plain sight.

Her phone fell from her hand.

This was it. Finally.

"You're not going to get away with it." She pressed down on the button and held the nozzle, aiming directly at the ring.

A low hum filled the room as the hose vibrated. Then a burst of bright-purple sparks shot out of the nozzle and enveloped Joseph's hand.

His eyes widened, and the slick smile crumbled.

Midnight pressed again. Violet light flooded the room, raging against the ring. It was working. It was—

No.

The light vanished into the ether as if it had never existed, leaving Joseph standing there. She let go of the weapon, and Rockstar fell to the side of her body as Joseph touched the ring on his finger and smirked.

"Too late," he said in a cool voice as his eyes snapped open, golden and bright. "I already have gotten away with it."

Chapter Sixteen

The ring wasn't the relic.

Midnight forced her gaze away from his finger and the golden blaze of his eyes. She quickly assessed her options. He was blocking the exit, but there was still plenty of room on either side of him, plus he was on crutches. She took a deep breath and zipped to the far left.

"Not so fast." He snapped his fingers, and an arc of golden flames burned the ground in front of her. Smoke rose from the carpet and she was forced back, coughing. Her heart pounded as she ran behind the floating body and past the wall of artifacts.

Another blast scorched the ground. Midnight let out a whimper of fear as she retreated. Her mind whirled.

If the ring wasn't the relic, then what was?

It couldn't be anything he had on his body, because surely the blast from Rockstar would've destroyed it. Which meant it was somewhere else.

"My friends will be here any minute," she warned as Joseph stepped toward her, letting the crutches fall to the ground. Her panic increased.

He wasn't just using planodiume to bring Eduardo De Rossi back to life; he'd also been using it for himself, healing his leg and his burns. So much for her advantage.

"I don't think so." He shook his head, golden eyes still blazing. "That boyfriend of yours was looking mighty cozy with another girl. And Tabitha...well... Let's just say she has other things on her mind right now."

"I don't believe you." Besides, he didn't know about the tracking button she'd pressed into the fabric of the tent. Her friends would be able to find it using their Pings. She just needed to buy some time.

"Yes, but you're twelve. What do *you* know?" He gave

her a dismissive wave. "You'll find out soon enough that people let you down."

"You're wrong." Midnight shook her head, trying not to think of Zelda's words. *You're not special.* "My friends would never let me down. They'll come."

"Even if they do, how can they help?" Joseph lifted both hands. Sparks of golden fire flew out of them, screeching, like nails against a blackboard. "They're insignificant and powerless. Just like you."

He was crazy.

"Do you have any idea how dangerous it is to use planodiume?" Midnight took a step back and tried to control her breathing. Joseph didn't seem to notice.

"Dangerous? I think you mean amazing. To feel raw power coursing through your veins is like nothing I've experienced. Not that you'd understand. I take it you're the ASP agent. I knew there'd be one here—at the most famous Black Stream in the world. Though I never guessed they'd give the job to a kid. Shows how useless they are. Still, I shouldn't complain. One less problem to deal with."

"If we're so easy to beat, how come we've stopped

two people from stealing planodiume in the last nine months?" Midnight retorted.

"Dumb luck?" Joseph shrugged, looking unbothered. "Not that it matters, because you're too late. Soon Eduardo De Rossi will be alive, and I'll have my reward. Power. Riches. Respect. Do you have any idea how humiliating it is to work for a buffoon like Carlo? To live like a pauper? For years I've worked just to get by. Well, that's all about to change."

"No." Midnight shook her head, thinking of all the people who'd been injured since the circus had arrived. "Please. You can't take so much life. It's not right."

"Now you sound like Carlo. Can you believe he refused to use Eduardo's journal? He kept it on the shelf of his trailer, too scared to touch it. It'd probably still be there if he hadn't told me about it. Fool. He thought I'd be as horrified as he'd been about his great-great-grandfather's dark past."

"So you stole the journal?"

"You say it like it's a bad thing." He shrugged. "You're as pathetic as Carlo. Too scared to try for anything great."

"He was right to be scared."

"Scared of power? Scared of being the best?" Joseph

raised his hands and sent another shower of lethal golden light up into the air. The chandelier shook.

"Scared of stealing people's lives from them."

He shrugged. "Most people squander their lives anyway. Too caught up in mundane things to even notice that the days and years are going by. I'm doing them a favor."

"You really believe that?"

"Of course. Look at the great things I can achieve. And when Eduardo's alive, nothing will be off limits."

"But you're not just stealing their lives, you're taking their memories," Midnight insisted. How could he not feel any remorse? "Carlo, Zelda, and everyone else you work with. They can't remember half the things that have happened because you've wiped their minds."

"That's what friends are for." He took another step closer and gave her a toothy smile. "Besides, they're used to it. This whole thing's been five years in the making."

"Five years?" Midnight tried to edge back toward the door.

"I started small at first. Worried the ASP might figure out what I was doing or that the relic wouldn't handle it. I needn't have worried. The ASP is a bunch of old women who don't have a clue what's going on."

Midnight's mouth was dry. "And the relic?"

"Ah. I see what you're doing." Joseph pointed a finger at her. "Trying to get me to tell you what it is, so you can destroy it with that weapon of yours."

Midnight winced. Logan would've figured out a way to get Joseph to admit what it was. Sweat beaded her brow. *Speaking of Logan.* Where was he? Where were both of her friends?

"I might already know," she bluffed.

"Correct. But it won't do you any good." He fixed his eyes on hers. His irises sparked with amber light. "You won't remember any of this. You'll forget you've seen me. Forget about Eduardo De Rossi. Then you'll send your friends into the tent so they can forget too. That's right," he said, his voice a low melodic purr, making him sound like some kind of hypnotist.

Midnight glared at him. As if she was going to follow any of his suggestions. Then she froze as understanding hit her.

He'd just tried to use mind control to wipe away her memories.

And it hadn't worked!

"I don't think so," she replied in a cool voice and was pleased to see his mouth drop open. "Seems you're not as good as you think you are."

"It's okay." He managed to collect himself. "Mind control might not have worked, but there's always plan B. It's a more permanent solution. Still, at least your death won't be wasted. I need another fifteen hundred and sixty years of life. Your twelve years will get me closer to my goal."

Twelve years? Did he mean…kill her?

He was going to kill her. And others. Midnight desperately tried to calculate how many people could die because she'd failed to stop him. But it was a blur. All she knew was that over fifteen hundred years was a lot of lives.

"No," she whimpered. "Please. You can't keep doing this."

"Actually, I can. And don't worry. The mind control might not have worked, but the spectral transference will. If it's any consolation, at least you'll die watching a great show."

Show?

Joseph lifted three glass orbs out of his pocket. A shriek of planodiume battered her ears as he threw the first orb into the air. He started to whistle.

He juggled faster, the golden light inside the balls growing brighter. Panic hit her. They were filled with the sickly energy. His whistling increased, and from across the room came a sniffing noise. As if something had been woken up.

A roar followed—low and deep like a thunderstorm—as the lion once again appeared in the cage. A tiger and an elephant soon followed, while the old-fashioned carousel horse began to slowly move up and down. Lights flashed, and carnival music added to the swirling confusion.

"Welcome to the show, Midnight." Joseph laughed as the orbs spun in the air. Then he let out a sharp whistle, and the cage doors all flew open.

The lion moved first. Its powerful jaws were stretched wide as it jumped forward and slashed at her with an enormous paw.

She stepped back, then screamed as the elephant raised its trunk and stormed from its cage. Her back pressed into the wall of the tent as sounds of the wild show blasted around her.

The room spun, and she sank to her knees just as buzzing noise filled the tent and pink fog flooded in.

Eliza.

The purple-tasseled cloth that'd been lying on the carpet near Eduardo De Rossi's floating body rose in the air like something from the ghost train ride. Then it flew directly into Joseph's face, momentarily blinding him. The chaotic scene instantly stopped.

Run.

She didn't know if it was a voice or a thought, but she didn't need to be told twice. The walls pounded like a heartbeat as she flew down the long corridor.

Eliza's pink form raced along next to her, urging her on until Midnight burst through the canvas flaps and back out into the bright daylight. After the chaotic frenzy of the tent, the world seemed still and quiet, and it took her a moment to regroup.

She needed to find her friends.

To warn them that they weren't safe, and to make sure they were well hidden from Joseph. His mind control hadn't worked on her, but Tabitha and Logan might not be immune.

Where were they?

She reached for her phone before remembering she'd dropped it in the tent. There was no way she could go back in there on her own. Not without a plan.

She ran toward the big top before coming to an abrupt halt.

The huge tent was surrounded by people all staring at scorched canvas while cloying smoke filled the air. Firefighters emerged from a gaping hole, their faces grim as ash and soot clung to their suits.

"Midnight, thank goodness. I've been looking for you everywhere." Akari hurried over, clutching Kiro's hand.

"You have? Is everything okay? Where's Logan?"

"He's with Tabitha," Akari said in a soft voice. "They've gone to the hospital."

What? Midnight's throat tightened, and her knees began to buckle.

"Are they okay? Are they hurt?"

"It's not them." Akari shook her head, her huge eyes filled with tears. "It's Tabitha's dad. The fire chief. One minute he was helping put out the fire, and then he just crumpled to the ground. No one knows what's wrong with him, but apparently he's in a coma."

"What?" The world began to spin. "That's not possible."

"Logan tried to call, but you weren't answering," Akari continued.

"I lost my phone," she said.

"He knew you'd be upset, which is why he wanted me to wait for you. He asked me to give you this." Akari held out a folded piece of paper. "Don't worry, I haven't looked at it."

"Thanks." Midnight unfolded the note, her hands trembling.

Midnight, it's bad.
Here is Mr. Wilson's Ping reading
SED: 88%
Life-Span Depletion: 58 years

Midnight closed her eyes.

This couldn't be happening. It couldn't be real.

Joseph said Tabitha "had some other things on her

mind right now." Which meant he'd known Mr. Wilson was in a coma. Because *he* was the one responsible for it.

"Are you okay?" Akari's voice seemed to come from far away.

Midnight slowly shook her head.

She wasn't okay. Not okay at all.

CHAPTER SEVENTEEN

"Is there any news on Mr. Wilson?" Midnight asked the moment she stepped out of the hospital elevator and hurried over to where Logan was sitting in the sterile waiting room. His face was grim as he stood up and shook his head.

"He hasn't regained consciousness, and no one but family can go in there," Logan said as he clutched at a house key in his hand. "Mrs. Wilson asked me to bring back some of Mr. Wilson's favorite things. My mom's coming to collect me."

Oh. Midnight numbly nodded. Logan's family lived

next door to the Wilsons, so that made sense. It was the only thing that made sense.

How could this be happening?

But she knew the answer to that. It was because she hadn't been able to stop Joseph.

She pushed a strand of hair back from her cheek. "I-is Tabitha's dad going to be okay?"

Logan took a deep breath. "It's not looking good. I don't think Joseph cares how much spectral energy he takes, as long as he gets what he needs. Did you find the ring? Because the sooner you destroy it—"

"The ring isn't the relic," Midnight croaked. "We were wrong. And before I could search for the relic, Joseph let the animals loose on me again. I only escaped because Eliza helped. Joseph said he needs fifteen hundred more years of energy."

Logan went pale. "And he needs it by tonight. That's why he took so much from Mr. Wilson. And he's probably going to do the same to everyone else at the circus. He doesn't care who he kills."

Horror filled Midnight. but she swallowed it down. "We have to stop him."

"I wish I could," Logan said. "But my mom's freaked out by everything that's happened. I'm not even sure if I'll be able to leave the house. You might need to do this one on your own. Because if you don't…"

The words trailed off. Unspoken.

Then Tabitha's dad could die. And so would other people. Probably everyone from the circus. For all she knew, they were already dead.

All so that one man could come back to life.

"What if I can't figure it out?" Midnight whispered.

"You can. You've got the tracker on the tent, so you'll be able to find it again, and the relic has to be somewhere inside," Logan said. "You could fire Rockstar at everything in there. A process of elimination."

Midnight swallowed. If only it were that simple.

"All the animals. The lights. The music. It was chaos. I could hardly move. Even if I knew what the relic was, I'm not sure I could get to it."

"You have to. I believe in you. So does Tabitha," Logan said as his phone beeped. He frowned. "It's my mom. She's waiting in the parking lot downstairs."

"Okay," Midnight said, trying not to think about the

blasts of golden fire the clown had thrown at her. That she'd only escaped because of Eliza. That everything she'd managed to do was with her friends by her side. "Tell Tabitha I won't let her down."

"I don't need to tell her, Midnight. She already knows."

"Thanks." She swallowed and made her way to the bus stop. Her limbs were like rocks, and it took all of her energy just to stand up. The bus was empty as she climbed onboard. Her mind was whirling. Logan was right. She had to keep searching.

The huge, looming shapes of the lion and elephant stampeded into her mind. Her flesh prickled, and a shiver raced down her spine.

"This is your stop." The driver's voice broke in, and Midnight looked up. They'd reached the circus. "Don't forget there's only one more bus coming this way, and it will be here in half an hour."

She forced herself to get off and watch the taillights disappear down the road.

The circus was deserted, and the fading daylight sent long shadows sweeping out in front of her. There were no signs of police or firefighters, just a huge metal fence blocking her out.

It hadn't been there earlier.

Had Joseph used planodiume to create it?

It had to be at least seven feet high, and there were sharp spikes running along the top, preventing anyone from climbing over. Midnight ran, looking for a way in, but the fence continued around the entire circus.

She peered between the metal bars for any sign of the performers who worked there, but there was nothing other than the occasional birdsong as evening descended.

She had to get in.

Her fingers tightened around the metal as the sound of a thousand bees slammed into her ears. A shower of golden sparks of light flew through the air from somewhere behind a tent. *Spectral transference.*

Then the sounds began. At first it was a faint whistle as Joseph appeared in the distance. Through the dim lights she could see the three glass orbs he was juggling, marking him like a beacon. And behind him was a procession of people. Carlo, Zelda, the woman who worked at the Laughing Clowns, Ryan...

Midnight tugged at the steel bars, but they were

unmoving, and all she could do was stare as Joseph led the procession like a modern-day pied piper.

So, it was true. He was going to get the energy he needed from the people who'd once been his friends. He obviously didn't care if they lived or died.

Help me, Eliza.

But there was no sign of the pink spirit that had come to her aid so many times in the past. Midnight ran along the fence again, looking for any way through. But each gate was firmly shut with a giant padlock. The sun finally fell from the sky as the last bus pulled up.

Midnight's shoulders slumped as she reluctantly walked over and climbed on. Zelda had been right. Midnight wasn't special. She was just a regular girl, and she hadn't been able to do it.

* * *

"Has there been any change in Mr. Wilson's condition?" her mom asked as Midnight trudged back into the house.

Her mom was wearing a traditionally dyed Viking dress that reached her feet, and there were leaves threaded through her hair. Behind her, Phil was in a leather vest and trousers with braids in his beard. In his hand was a platter of raw vegetables that looked like they were going to be roasted in the fire pit he'd built at the back of the garden.

Midnight had forgotten all about the summer solstice party. A car rumbled to a halt in the driveway. Several Vikings spilled out, laughing and shouting as they walked toward the fire pit.

"No change." She shook her head and willed herself not to cry. "Logan's going to let me know as soon as he hears anything."

"Oh, sweetheart." Her mom wrapped her in a hug. "I feel so bad. Should we cancel the party? It doesn't seem right."

"It's okay." Midnight shook her head. Truth was that she'd rather be alone. Whoever said misery loved company was lying. Her mom didn't look convinced, but Phil just gave Midnight's shoulder a gentle touch.

"If you need a lift to the hospital—or anything at all—just let us know."

"I will." Midnight swallowed, and after assuring her mom several more times she was okay, she headed up the stairs.

Tears pricked in the corners of her eyes.

She'd taken so much for granted. Her mom. Phil. Her friends. Even Eliza. They all did things for her, but when Tabitha needed her the most, Midnight couldn't help.

As she passed Taylor's bedroom, she could hear Rita snuffling and running about, but Midnight kept walking. Her sister was still struggling to deal with what had happened to her the last time Midnight battled planodiume; she didn't need to be freaked out more.

Midnight dropped her backpack onto the floor. Her laptop was sitting open on the desk. Without her phone, she hadn't been able to call Logan. She sent him a message, but after she stared at the screen for ten minutes, there still was no reply.

He was probably back at the hospital.

Too busy trying to help Tabitha and her mom.

Joseph had won.

Midnight shut her laptop and stood up.

Normally she loved looking at her spreadsheets, using them to create order in her life, but what was the point when she couldn't even get back into the circus?

She pushed away the pages of research notes, and they fell to the floor. All their theories landed near her feet. By her chair were the numerous sketches she'd made, and along with the pages was the thin piece of golden rope.

Midnight left them all there. What was the point?

Brrrring.

The sound of the doorbell rang in her ear.

There was no way her mom would've heard it from out by the fire pit, and since Taylor hardly seemed to leave her room, Midnight doubted her sister would answer it.

It was either one of her mom's friends, or the neighbors complaining about the noise. Midnight reluctantly walked downstairs and swung open the door to where Tyson Carl was standing.

His blond hair was tied back, and he was wearing the same black hoodie he'd been wearing at Dingle Donuts.

"H-hey," she said, not able to hide her surprise. "I didn't expect you."

He pushed back a strand of hair and chewed his lip. "I tried to call, but you didn't answer."

Because my phone's stuck in an invisible tent where an evil clown is killing people.

"It's a long story," she said, not quite sure what to do. "Everything okay?"

"Not really." He shook his head as his shoulders sagged. "I heard about Tab's dad, but they wouldn't let me see her at the hospital. Plus, Logan's mom has him on lockdown. I'm going nuts, and…well…I don't really know why I came here. I should go. It sounds like you're having—" He frowned, obviously not quite sure what to make of the noise coming from the back of the house.

"It's a Viking party." Midnight loosened her grip on the door. She might not know Tyson that well, but she knew exactly how he was feeling. The frustration. The sense of helplessness. "Do you want to come in for a bit?"

"Are you sure?" Uncertainty flashed across his face, probably thanks to the huge guy dressed in gleaming chain mail who poked his head out from the kitchen to see what was going on.

"Yeah." She turned to the Viking. "It's okay. It's just a friend." Then she nodded to Tyson. "We should probably go to my room unless you want to learn how to dance like a Viking and eat pickled food."

Tyson's eyes widened, and he quickly followed Midnight up the stairs just as Taylor's door opened enough for Rita to bounce toward them. Her little nose twitched as she sniffed Tyson's leg before looking up at him, huge eyes like deep pools of water.

"Hey." He bent down and patted her, much to Rita's delight. "You're adorable. I didn't know you had a puppy."

"She's not ours. We're just dog-sitting her while her owner's away," Midnight said as Rita wagged her tail and followed them into the bedroom. The small puppy began to play with the scattered sheets of paper that littered the floor. Midnight didn't bother to stop her. She didn't even care if Tyson saw them and figured out what she'd been doing.

The normal panic of having someone discover her secret was gone. It just didn't seem to matter anymore.

"You can sit if you want." She gestured to the chair at her desk. Tyson slumped into it, his long legs stretching out in front of him, while Midnight perched on the corner of her bed. Rita made a snuffling noise as she continued to bounce from one piece of paper to the next.

"Were you with Tabitha when the accident happened?" he suddenly asked, and Midnight winced, not wanting to talk about their fight—especially the part that involved him.

"I was in a different part of the circus. Then I lost my phone, and by the time I found out, they were already at the hospital," she said, and the room fell silent. Finally Tyson let out a deep sigh.

"My dad died when I was five. It's just me, my mom, and my older sister. I really hope Mr. Wilson's okay."

"Me too," Midnight said in a whisper. "My dad died when I was little so I don't remember him. But now that I've got a stepdad, I'd hate to not have one around again."

"I just wish there was something I could do," Tyson said as another Viking roar went up from the yard. Midnight tugged at a frayed thread on her shorts, and Tyson suddenly said, "I know you saw me at Dingle Donuts the other day. When that car got broken into."

"Oh." Her face heated, and she forgot about the loose thread. "I should've said hi, but you…well…you seemed distracted. I didn't want to get in your way." As far as excuses went, it was lame, but Tyson seemed to accept it.

He let out another sigh. "It wouldn't have mattered anyway. Man. Everything's so messed up."

"What do you mean? What's going on?"

"Nothing." He shook his head. "Nothing you'd understand. But hey, thanks for not telling Tabitha. I know how dodgy it must've looked to see me hanging out in the parking lot when I was meant to be at my grandma's. I was sick all night, worrying what you might've said to her. Like that I was no good for her."

Midnight shut her eyes. She wanted to tell him she wasn't that kind of person. The kind of person who judged. But she couldn't. Because she *had* judged him, even if she hadn't told Tabitha.

"Don't thank me," she said, guilt catching in her words. "I should be apologizing to you. I didn't tell her, but I thought about it, even though I had no idea what you were doing. I should've just asked."

Tyson gave her a frank smile. "I probably wouldn't have told you. I was pretty upset. Things have been bad lately. Mom lost her job, and money's been tight. To make it worse, Libby's been dating a complete loser. Once when he was at the house, I heard him boasting that he'd been breaking into cars and stealing stuff."

Midnight sat up. Taylor had mentioned that Donna and Libby had been hanging out with a bad bunch.

"That's what you were doing there. You were following him?"

He nodded. "I wanted to get some proof to show her. My mom's got enough worries on her plate, and now she's not sleeping because she's freaked that Libby will end up in trouble."

"I'm so sorry." Midnight's eyes filled with understanding. Up until they'd moved to Berry, her mom had always been broke, always worried about money, and it was something Midnight had been teased about for most of her life. Well, that and the name, obviously. She looked up at him. "Did it work? Did you get the proof?"

"I did." He gave her a reluctant smile. "And not only did she dump the loser, but she took the evidence to the police. That was this morning, and I was just starting to think I could enjoy the rest of the summer. Hang out with you guys. Go on some more dates with Tab. Then Logan told me about the accident…"

He trailed off, and they were both silent as the reality seeped back into the room. Finally he stood up.

"I should go. It's looks like you're in the middle of something," he said as Rita started to bark at one of the pieces of paper, nudging it with her nose, like she did with her leash. "Is she okay?"

Midnight sighed. "Yeah. She probably just wants a thing that starts with a *W*. I'll take her out after you leave."

"Sure," he said and glanced down at the mess on the floor. "What are those drawings, anyway? Some kind of whip?"

"No." She followed his gaze to the numerous sketches she'd made of the snake on the De Rossi gravestone. She couldn't tell where the face and tail of the snake had been. She supposed they'd been chipped away with age. "It's not a whip. It's a—"

She gasped.

They'd just assumed the object on the headstone was a snake because at first they'd been looking for a snake. But Joseph had lied about the snake to mislead them.

So what if the thing on the gravestone wasn't a snake at all?

Was it possible?

Her pulse hammered. "Do you really think it's a whip?"

"Well, yeah. Look." He pointed to one of the circus flyers hanging on her wall. The picture of Eduardo De

Rossi. In one hand was a megaphone, and in the other was a whip. A *golden* whip. "And this looks like a piece of leather from it."

He plucked up the scrap of golden rope they'd found outside the ghost train after the accident. It was still in the plastic evidence bag where she'd put it. After they'd discovered Joseph was responsible, they hadn't bothered to find out anything else about it, since it hadn't seemed important.

Midnight's mouth opened and then closed again, and Tyson passed it over to her.

She rubbed it with the tip of her finger. The golden paint flecked away to reveal the rough edge of leather.

She blinked, and her eyes slowly began to see a coiled whip where moments before there had only been a coiled snake.

It all added up.

It had been right in front of her the entire time.

"Thank you," she said.

"Thanks for what?" His face wrinkled with confusion. He had no idea what he'd just done. That he might've just saved the day.

Now she knew what the relic was. Now she could go back to the circus…

Her mind whirled.

Except there were no more buses. To get to the circus, she'd need someone to drive her. Taylor might be able to do it. But it wasn't enough. There was still the fence to get over.

Tyson shifted from foot to foot, and Midnight swallowed. Could he help her? Tabitha had accused Midnight of not trusting him. And her friend had been right.

But that didn't mean she couldn't change her mind. He'd been honest with her. More importantly, he'd shown how far he'd go for people he cared about. Plus he was Logan's best friend. If she couldn't trust him with her secret, then who could she trust?

She took a deep breath. "You said you wished there was something you could do to help Tabitha's dad. Did you mean it?"

"Of course." He was immediately beside her, his face drawn and serious. "Anything."

"Okay." She gave him a shy smile. "How do you feel about doing some breaking and entering?"

"If you think it will work, then I feel surprisingly good about it," he said as Midnight hurried down the hallway and banged on Taylor's door. She could explain everything on the way, but if they stood a chance, they had to leave now. And that meant Taylor would need to drive.

Midnight wasn't going to take no for an answer.

Chapter Eighteen

"You can see ghosts?" Tyson asked as Taylor took the corner at five miles an hour. Rita made little panting noises from her puppy cage. This wasn't quite how Midnight had planned for it to go, but at least Taylor had agreed to drive.

Their mom had hardly even listened to their excuse of a late-night frozen-yogurt run. She was just happy Taylor was leaving the house. The only thing Midnight hadn't counted on was her sister's insistence that Rita come along. After all, it wasn't exactly safe for any of them, let alone a little puppy. Taylor had argued that leaving Rita around a bunch of marauding Vikings wasn't much better.

"Spectral energy is more like multicolored snowflakes," she explained before leaning forward to her sister. "Can you at least drive at the speed limit?"

"Don't interrupt me. I need to concentrate," Taylor said in a curt voice but at the same time increased the speed by a fraction.

"And you can only see it when you're wearing those glasses?" Tyson continued, his voice filled with awe. His reaction had been similar to Logan and Tabitha's. It also proved she'd been right to trust him.

"Yes. Though for some reason, Joseph's mind control doesn't work on me, which is why I'm the one who needs to go into the tent and get the whip."

"I still can't believe this is your job. And that Tabitha and Logan have been helping you." Tyson ran a hand through his hair.

"I'm sorry if you felt left out," Midnight said before Taylor finally came to a halt outside Tyson's house. It was neat and tidy, though the wood needed painting and the gutter was sagging at one end.

"Trust me, I get what it's like to worry about what people think of you." He nodded at the modest house. "I'll only be a couple of minutes. My dad was a builder, and my mom's never been able to sell his tools. I'm sure we have a bolt cutter."

Tyson had suggested using one to get through the heavy chain on the gate, which was why they'd made the detour.

"Hey, if you see Libby while you're in there, tell her we should hang out sometime," Taylor said, sounding more like her old self.

"I will," he replied and scrambled out of the car, leaving the two sisters alone. Rita let out a little bark, and Taylor craned her neck.

"She might be nervous."

"She seems okay." Midnight lifted the little puppy out to cuddle her.

"Lucky her." Taylor shivered, sending a rush of guilt through Midnight.

"I'm sorry you had to drive. If I called a taxi at this time of night, Mom might've freaked out. I know you're scared."

For a moment Taylor was silent. "I guess that's the whole point."

"What do you mean?" Midnight stroked Rita's fur, and the little puppy licked her fingers.

"After what happened with Dylan, I was petrified of ever being in this position again." Her sister stared out into the night as if caught up in the memory.

"Taylor, there's nothing wrong with that. He tried to *kill* you. Being scared is normal. Besides, it wasn't your fault. It was mine. If I'd gotten to him sooner. If I'd—"

"Midnight, stop. What I meant was that even though I was terrified, I kind of took it for granted that because you can see spectral energy, somehow it made you braver. But I get it now."

"Get what?" Midnight leaned forward while Rita continued to lick her finger.

"I get that no matter how scared you are, you keep going out and trying to make things better. I get that what makes you special is not what you can see, but what you do about it. Even when it's terrifying."

Midnight opened her mouth, then shut it again as her eyes prickled with tears. She'd never thought of it like that. Before she could reply, Rita pawed the frames of her glasses and licked them. The lenses steamed up.

"Hey, I'm going to need them tonight," Midnight protested. She pushed her frames back up her face as Tyson reappeared with a large canvas bag.

"Got it."

Midnight put Rita back into the traveling cage as Taylor turned the car back on and pulled out into the night. The three of them were silent on the short trip, and when they finally arrived, Midnight's hands were shaking.

"Where's the best place to get in?" Taylor picked up Rita's cage and joined them. The small puppy started to bark before Taylor took a tattered old T-shirt out of her purse and slid it through the cage. Rita was immediately silent. Midnight had a funny feeling it was her sister's favorite Twenty One Pilots shirt.

"The gate," Tyson said as he tugged his black hood over his pale-blond hair.

"Is there any"—Taylor paused and looked around— "planodiume?"

"I can't see any right now," Midnight said, not sure whether that was a good thing or a bad thing. It might mean Joseph was just taking a break…or it might mean that she was too late.

"All the more reason to get in there quickly." Tyson lifted the bolt cutters out of the bag. The flat nose was a dull, dark metal, but the orange handles were bright against the night. He lifted them up to the giant chain wrapped around the gate. His arms strained and his jaw clenched, but then there was a sharp click and the chain clattered to the ground. The gate swung open.

The three of them glanced around as if expecting someone to race over to see what the noise was, but it was silent.

Because everyone was with Joseph in the tent, where he was going to kill them and steal their spectral energy.

"What now?" Taylor's voice was laced with fear. Midnight held up her Ping, and a map appeared on the screen. The device emitted a soft *ping, ping*.

"There's a tracker on the tent," she said before looking at Tyson, Taylor, and Rita. "But you both need to stay here. I don't want anything to happen to you guys."

"If Tabitha and Logan were here, would they go with you?" Tyson asked.

"It's kind of hard to stop them," Midnight admitted. "But…they know what they're up against."

"So do I," Taylor said in a low but firm voice. Rita barked in agreement.

"Shouldn't we call the police?" Tyson frowned.

"There's nothing they can do. They can't even see spectral energy, let alone make a law against it."

Tyson didn't look happy. "So anyone you don't catch just gets away with it?"

"More or less," Midnight agreed. "But that's not going to happen. Not tonight. And if you're both coming, you have to promise not to come into the tent. You might still be affected by his mind control."

Taylor looked like she was going to protest before finally nodding. "You're the boss."

"Thanks." Midnight set her mouth into a tight grimace as she held up her Ping and headed for the tent.

The moon was partially concealed by clouds, and the giant rides were like sleeping animals, casting shadows as Midnight, Tyson, and Taylor walked through the deserted circus. In the distance, a whistle sounded, and once again golden light split the sky. Midnight lowered her Ping. She didn't need the tracker at all. The planodiume Joseph was stealing would do that for her.

She increased her pace and turned left at a hot dog cart before coming to a stop outside the faded purple tent. Taylor gave it a skeptical glare.

"How can everyone be in there? It's the size of a bus stop."

"I can't explain it." Midnight opened her backpack and carefully lifted the amplifier-shaped weapon out.

"Is that what will destroy the whip?" Tyson swept a skeptical gaze over the weapon. Even Taylor looked a bit concerned.

"In theory." Midnight slipped it over her shoulder and tightened her grip on the slim nozzle.

But first she had to *find* the whip.

She gave her sister and Tyson one last look and stepped into the tent.

The corridor was pitch-black, and the only sound was the soft pad of her shoes against the carpet as she walked down it. The silence was shattered by a soft whistle, and she stiffened as she reached the main chamber.

The glittering lights of the chandelier was gone, and the entire room was dark, apart from a spotlight trained directly on the center of the tent. Despite the gloom, Midnight could see people seated all around the outside of the ring, a captive audience. Their eyes were filled with gold and their expressions blank.

"Don't be shy." A figure stepped into the spotlight.

It was Joseph. He was wearing an immaculate tuxedo. His blue wig was gone, and his hair was a waterfall of thick brown curls. The only color on his entire person was the grotesque red clown smile painted onto his mouth.

He whistled and slowly threw a golden orb into the air, closely followed by a second and then a third.

"You're not going to get away with this," Midnight said, searching through the darkness for the golden whip. Joseph was just trying to distract her. She had to ignore him.

"You're funny. Not as funny as me, of course. But then hey, I'm a clown."

The orbs tore through the air faster and faster as the spotlight grew wider. Joseph turned to his left and smiled at something. "Look, Eduardo. It's the girl I told you about. I was hoping she'd turn up for the show."

The spotlight widened to reveal the body of Eduardo De Rossi. The shimmering figure she'd seen was gone, replaced by a solid body. It was still floating in the air, tied down to the table with thin golden straps.

"So I see." The figure slowly sat up, and several of the golden straps snapped. Midnight came face-to-face with the former ringmaster.

His skin was the color of alabaster, while a flowing mustache ran down his chin and his raven locks fell in glossy curls to his shoulder. A couple of patches on his neck still shimmered with golden light, but as Joseph continued to juggle, they slowly filled up.

Midnight bit back a scream and turned to the captive audience. She could just make out the gleam of Zelda's jewelry. A glimmer of recognition sparkled in the fortune-teller's eyes.

"Zelda. Please, you have to get everyone out."

"I don't think so," Joseph interrupted as he juggled faster.

"Don't kill her. Having someone who can see spectral energy will be useful. I think she can come with us." Eduardo's voice was a low purr that sent a shiver racing down Midnight's spine.

"Might be a problem. The control doesn't work on her. I've already tried."

"Ah, yes. But that doesn't mean it can't be done." A horrifying smile spread out across Eduardo's face. "I didn't leave all my secrets in the journal."

She stiffened. She'd assumed she must be immune to the mind control, but it seemed Joseph didn't have the skills to do it properly.

Unlike Eduardo.

"You sly dog." Joseph widened his eyes before grinning. "Even more reason to get on with the show."

The orbs in his hands moved ever faster, and the dissonant sound of an organ filled the tent. The glittering chandelier flickered to life, bathing the entire room in light.

Finally. She could see.

She spun around to the far wall where all the circus memorabilia had been stored. There was no sign of the whip. Panic caught in her throat. What if she'd come all this way for nothing?

She rubbed her brow as a faint bark echoed out.

Rita?

There it was again. It was coming from behind one of

the posters. She frowned as the little puppy's black-and-white head appeared from behind it, the golden whip clutched firmly in her mouth. She was wagging her tail, as if eagerly waiting to be taken on a walk.

She'd found it!

"Good girl." Midnight ran toward Rita, but before she could reach the little dog, Joseph let out a sharp whistle and was answered by an ear-shattering roar that reverberated around the tent—and the giant lion appeared.

No!

The ground shuddered as a slate-gray elephant stormed around the circumference of the tent, its trunk sweeping back and forth like a violent broom.

Wind whipped, sharp and jagged, while bolts of golden energy streamed into the floating body of Eduardo De Rossi. A couple of angry monkeys appeared in front of the lion, their outraged chattering only adding to the chaotic scene.

Rita let out a terrified bark, and Midnight's mouth went dry. The puppy might not be able to see the animals, but she could obviously sense something was wrong. Very, very wrong.

The little puppy began to shake. Midnight tried to move, but her feet refused to respond. She was anchored to the spot as the lion roared and shook its mane before stepping toward her.

Last time, she'd barely escaped the deadly claw as it had swiped at her.

"Move. Rita needs you. Mr. Wilson needs you." She screamed the words out loud, hoping to shock herself into action. It worked, and she managed to jump away before the lion could reach her.

The elephant trumpeted its anger and charged. Midnight scurried in the other direction, trying her best to reach the frightened puppy and the golden whip. But it was no good. The monkeys let out a furious hiss and raced for her. Almost as though they were trying to herd her back into the path of the wild beasts.

Rita let out another terrified bark.

Eduardo De Rossi might not want her dead, but Joseph seemed to have other ideas. She clamped down on her lower lip to keep from crying.

The golden whip was only twenty feet away.

Twenty feet between her and the lives of so many people.

In the distance was a flash of movement as Zelda—*and Taylor?*—herded the captive audience toward the exit. Though the only way they'd really escape from this madness was if Midnight could destroy the whip.

"Eliza." She screamed the name into the air, and a blast of pink fog swept into the tent. "Please, you have to help me get past them. It's the only way."

"I don't know who you're talking to, but it won't work," Joseph howled through the chaos as he threw the golden orbs higher. He snapped his fingers, and a person perched on a flying trapeze flashed past her, the knife they were wielding slashing the air next to Midnight's ear. "You think you're special, but you're not."

She jumped back just in time, and the spirit of Eliza Irongate darted toward her, covering Midnight's face in pink fog. Unlike planodiume, there was nothing chilling in the touch. Instead, it was so warm that her glasses fogged up.

"What are you doing? I don't understand." Midnight used her sleeve to rub at her lenses, trying to improve her vision. It didn't work. "I can't take my glasses off, or else I'll be blind. I won't be able to—"

The words froze on her lips.

Without her glasses, she couldn't see planodiume *but* she wasn't helpless. She could still feel it. She was *still* herself. What had Zelda told her about the spectral energy at the circus?

If you're smart, you'll not see it either.

Understanding hit her.

Zelda hadn't been trying to scare her; she'd been trying to warn her. Because if she couldn't see the phantom creatures, they couldn't hurt her. Joseph didn't have as much power as he thought. Eduardo had even told him so. He'd said he hadn't left all of his tricks in the journal.

All Joseph could do was create illusions. They weren't real. Eduardo could obviously do a lot more. If he'd been fully alive, the animals in the tent might've been real. The power he used to control minds would've been even more intense.

But Eduardo wasn't fully alive yet. Which meant Midnight was only dealing with Joseph and his phantom circus.

He was relying on her fear. Relying on the fact she wouldn't dare step through a lion and its sharp teeth.

And he was right. No one in their right mind would do that, not even if the phantom lion couldn't hurt them.

But without her glasses, Midnight wouldn't be able to see what Joseph had created.

Peter Gallagher had told her she was going in blind, but probably hadn't realized just how right he was.

"I understand," she whispered. The pink fog shot from the tent as Midnight lifted her hand and carefully took off her glasses.

A plain purple tent stared back at her.

Gone were the rampaging beasts, the wild music, the flickering chandelier. To her left was Joseph wearing his hobo costume, his blue wig matted and dirty, while next to him the floating body of Eduardo De Rossi was only tethered to the ground by two more golden straps.

There was still time.

You're not special, Midnight Reynolds.

Joseph blinked, and his juggling faltered. "Why did you take off the glasses? You're blind without them."

"Fool." Eduardo's voice was sharp. "She's not blind. She's still a protector. Don't let her get the relic."

"Too late." Midnight's lungs filled with air, and

without stopping to think about the dangers that had been there only moments earlier, she ran to the other side of the tent. Adrenaline pumped through her legs as she hurtled past Joseph.

Rita yapped with joy and darted toward her. Midnight scooped up the tiny puppy in one hand as the golden whip loomed in front of her. Bright as a new penny. She was so close now.

Ten steps, nine, eight. Rockstar was slung over her shoulder, her finger hovering over the inauspicious button. Seven, six, five…

"*Noooo!*" Joseph screamed from somewhere behind her, as if suddenly realizing what had happened. Midnight tuned him out. She pressed the button, and a piercing howl filled the air. She did it again, and the howl increased as purple light exploded from the slim nozzle.

The shimmering flash of energy arced up in the air and devoured the golden whip. *Crack.* The splintering noise filled the air, closely followed by a snap, but the violet-tinged light continued to swamp it.

She pressed the button again.

Rita trembled in her arm, but Midnight held her tight.

There was a second crack, this time fainter as Joseph reached her side.

"Stop it." He tried to drag Rockstar off her shoulder, but something made him scream, and his hands flew to his face as if he was being attacked by bees. Without her glasses, Midnight couldn't tell what it was.

It didn't matter. All that mattered was destroying the relic.

She tightened her grip on Rockstar's slim nozzle as more and more energy surged through the whip. Finally it stopped, and Midnight took a shaky step back, almost bumping into Taylor, who was now next to her.

"I told you to stay outside." Midnight panted.

"Rita managed to get out of her travel cage. I came in to find her and realized how many people were stuck in here. I couldn't just leave them, so I helped get them out. Don't worry, they're all safe. Did it work?" Taylor's face was no longer drained of color. It was pink. Like she was…*excited*?

Rita barked in answer, but Midnight fumbled with her glasses. "I don't know," she admitted as she pressed the frames up her nose. A stream of golden light flooded out of the whip, rising up through the top of the tent like a fountain. It was beautiful.

Midnight spun back to face Eduardo De Rossi. He was still sitting in the middle of the room.

His mouth was open as if he was trying to scream, but there were no words.

He was frozen, as the light was being dragged from his body, spiraling up to the ceiling and bursting back into the world.

Piece by piece, fragments of light were sucked from his body, turning him from gold to opaque. Then, as a soft breeze meandered through the tent, the last of the fragments vanished, and Eduardo De Rossi was no more.

"No. Stop it! My work." Joseph screeched as he ran to tackle her. But instead of him stepping forward, his knee buckled and he fell to the ground screaming in pain.

His broken leg!

Without the stolen planodiume, he could no longer walk.

"Midnight. You did it!" Taylor let out a whoop, which didn't quite fit either version of her sister. Midnight's knees began to knock as she slowly turned around.

"How do you know?"

"Because that's the same smile you get when Mom lets you meet Logan at Cookies and Cakes." Her sister grinned before nodding over to where Joseph was crumpled on the ground. "And look at him. It's like he's aged a hundred years."

It was true.

Beneath the clown makeup, deep lines were etched into Joseph's sullen cheeks as sirens split the night.

The police?

"I called them." Tyson came running into the tent. He was holding a phone up to his ear, and in his other hand was what looked like a memory stick. He gave her an apologetic smile. "I know you told me to stay hidden, but the idea of Joseph getting away with what he's done really bugged me. So, I found some proof."

"You don't understand. ASP's job is to keep spectral energy hidden from the world. People would freak out if they know it's true. We can't tell the police anything."

"Yeah, that's what Tabitha's been trying to tell me," Tyson said with a small grin. "Lucky the evidence I found was tapes of Joseph stealing money from other people in the circus. Not to mention setting the big top on fire while Mr. Wilson was in there. Oh, and speaking of Tabitha, she wants to talk to you."

"She's on the phone? Why didn't you tell me?" Midnight took it from his outstretched hand. Then she froze. Eduardo De Rossi was gone, but what if it had been too late? What if—

"Midnight," Tabitha yelled from the other end of the phone. "It's okay. My dad's okay."

"He is?" Midnight dared to lift the phone closer to her ear. "Are you sure?"

"I'm sure. The doctors can't figure out how he woke up completely fine, with no organ failure or anything. They're making him stay overnight to monitor him. But I swear he's one hundred percent back to normal. He threatened to take me on a father-daughter fun run," Tabitha said in disgust.

"A fun run?" Midnight burst out laughing as her panic and terror finally disappeared.

"Right," Tabitha said, though she didn't sound mad. Just relieved. "Seriously, thank you so much. My mom and I thought he was going to—"

"Don't even say it." Midnight cut her off. "I'm just pleased it worked. Tab, I was so scared."

"That makes two of us. But I knew you'd do it."

"I wish I'd had your confidence," Midnight admitted. "Plus I felt so bad about our fight. I'm so sorry about the things I said. If it wasn't for Tyson—"

"Hey," Taylor cut in with a cough while Rita gave a sharp bark. Midnight laughed.

"If it wasn't for Tyson, Taylor, Rita, *and* Eliza, I wouldn't have managed," she said before telling her best friend everything that had happened, from Eliza fogging up her glasses to Rita finding the golden whip. She even told her about Zelda's dire warning.

Tabitha listened in silence before she finally spoke. "I think Zelda meant that it's not your special abilities that makes you such a great protector, it's because you're you. It's regular Midnight who didn't want anything to happen to my dad, and who was worried about Taylor being freaked out. And who took the time to speak to Tyson. I think regular Midnight is kind of awesome."

Midnight opened her mouth but had no idea what to say. She was saved from having to respond as the police and paramedics flooded into the purple tent, which suddenly seemed far too small.

The phantom circus had gone, and all that was left was a furious Joseph. Midnight said a quick goodbye as the police surrounded the disgruntled clown.

"You can't do this," Joseph screamed as the paramedics put him on a stretcher. "That girl's crazy. She sees ghosts. And she talks to them."

"Sure she does," the first police officer said, his eyes narrowing. "Don't think I haven't read your file, buddy. Aliens, conspiracy theories, UFO sightings. Along with all the other charges, at least five states want to prosecute you for crank calls."

"That's different." Joseph tried to protest, but the police officer just nodded for the paramedics to trolley him out. He then turned to Midnight, Taylor, and Tyson.

"I'm not sure what you kids are doing here at this time of night. Regardless of the evidence you've given us, you're still technically trespassing."

"Not trespassing; they're here as my special guests." Carlo De Rossi walked in. His washed-out skin was gone, and he looked younger and happier than when

Midnight had first met him. He was followed by Zelda, who was just as bright and refreshed.

"Yes, we'd planned to put on a show for them, before—" Zelda's smile faltered as she nodded in the direction Joseph had been taken. "Well, before it was interrupted."

The police officer looked from Carlo to Zelda before shrugging. "If you're sure you don't want to press charges, we'll be on our way."

"And we'd better be going as well." Taylor held up her phone. "Mom's just sent a text. She wants to know why it's taking so long to get frozen yogurt. Here I was thinking I'd get a free pass for the rest of the summer."

"Before you go, I'd just like to say thank you," Carlo said in a low voice. "I can't remember everything, but Zelda's been filling me in. It seems she managed to fight Joseph's control and was aware of what was happening."

"Is that why you gave me that message?" Midnight said in surprise. "That if I'm smart, I won't see it either? And that I wasn't special?"

Zelda nodded. "Joseph was strong enough to stop me from saying anything to endanger what he was doing, but my visions are often cryptic, so that was the only way I could tell you that you were immune to those creatures he created."

Tabitha had been right. Then again, her friend wasn't often wrong.

"What's going to happen to Eduardo's journal?" Carlo asked as he picked up the leather book Joseph had been clutching.

"The people I work for will make sure it's safe," Midnight promised, relieved that soon it would be in the hands of Peter and the ASP team.

"Good." Carlo took a small box out of his pocket. "If you could give them this as well. It's Antonio's wedding ring. When I first found the journal, I hid the ring, thinking that would be enough. I didn't realize Eduardo's original whip could also be used as a relic."

The ring.

So they'd been right after all!

"Thank you," Midnight said as she glanced to her sister and Tyson. "I'd better get going. There's still a month left of my summer break. No way do I want to spend it being grounded."

"Grounded? Midnight, you're a superhero. I'm sure you won't get grounded," Carlo said.

"Actually." She grinned, taking off her glasses. "I'm just a regular girl. It took me awhile to figure it out."

Woof. Rita barked as she wriggled in Taylor's arms. They all burst out laughing. Then they said their good-byes and headed home. Now that she was just a regular girl, Midnight needed to do what everyone else did. Catch up on some sleep.

Epilogue

"No, Rita. Don't eat it." Bella squealed as the puppy wagged her tail and nuzzled at the pink ball Logan's little sister had thrown across the park.

"I don't know who's having more fun, Bella or Rita," Tabitha said as she brushed away the crumbs of a vegan cherry brownie and groaned. "I'm so full."

"Then perhaps you shouldn't have eaten three brownies in a row." Midnight stretched her legs out. Beams of pale buttery sunshine warmed her skin, and she smiled. Tabitha was sitting next to her, while Tyson and Logan were a little to the left, keeping an eye on Bella and talking about a movie they'd recently watched.

"Not my fault your mom lets me taste all the things on her new menu." Tabitha didn't look very repentant as she smoothed down her shiny black hair. The blue streak had been replaced by a red one, to celebrate her dad being okay.

It had been two weeks since Midnight had found the golden whip and stopped Joseph, and things were finally starting to settle down, especially now that ASP agents had come to Berry and spent a day checking out the circus and talking to Carlo to ensure nothing like that ever happened again.

"Tomorrow she's making vegan cinnamon rolls," Midnight said. The café had just opened and was already doing a booming business, in part helped by Tyson's mom, who was the new hostess and doing an amazing job. "She promised to save you some."

"Yes." Tabitha let out a rare smile before turning to face her. "So…have you spoken to him yet?"

"Oh." Midnight gulped and glanced over at Logan, who was laughing at something Tyson had said. "Not exactly. I'm not even sure what to say."

"How about, 'Hey, Logan. Sorry I got jealous of Akari. Especially since she's dating an exchange student from Norway.'"

"Stop making it sound so easy." Midnight took off her glasses and rubbed them. There'd been so much going on between the circus leaving town and her mom's new café that she'd hardly spent any time alone with Logan.

If this was what being a regular girl was like, she wasn't a fan.

"No, Rita. Don't eat rainbow bear." Bella squealed again as the puppy sniffed at the ugly toy Logan had won. Rita seemed to understand and let go of the bear.

Another change was that Rita's owner had decided to move to California to take care of her brother and wasn't allowed to have a pet in her apartment complex. Which meant the puppy was now a permanent member of Midnight's family. Something they were all happy about. Well, not Tabitha, but Midnight was sure her friend would eventually warm to Rita.

"Oh, hey. We've got to fly." Tabitha scrambled to her feet. "My dad's so excited I have a sporty boyfriend that he's challenged Tyson to a game of golf. Please, kill me now."

But despite the eye rolls, Tabitha seemed pretty happy.

"You might not hate it." Tyson joined them. "It's actually just like visiting the cemetery. Lots of walking and thinking, plus you might get to see the ghost of the original owner. Apparently she's still waiting for her husband at the fifteenth hole."

"Wait… It's a haunted golf course?" Tabitha's eyes widened. "Why did no one ever tell me this?"

"Because not all people get excited at the idea of ghosts?" Logan suggested, though his eyes were twinkling. "Or, should I say spectral energy."

"Their loss," Tabitha retorted as she gave Midnight a hug. "And don't forget we're meeting tomorrow at your mom's café to talk about the new weapon ASP sent you."

"Don't worry, it's in my spreadsheet," Midnight promised as Tabitha whispered "good luck" in her ear before walking toward the bus stop and out of sight.

Midnight waited until they were gone before turning back the picnic rug in time to see Bella and Rita both curled up fast asleep.

"Thanks for letting her meet the puppy." Logan nodded for Midnight to join him on the park bench next to the rug. "Ever since I told her about Rita, she's been dying to have a playdate."

"Of course. Besides, now that Taylor's no longer a hermit, I've been the one keeping her entertained. It's nice to have a break." Midnight sat down. "It's funny to think that nowhere in my summer plans was caring for a puppy or stopping a dead ringmaster from coming back to life."

"It's been a strange summer, that's for sure," Logan agreed before studying his knuckles as if he didn't know what to say next.

Midnight sucked in a breath of air. Tabitha was right. She just had to tell him she'd made a mistake. That she was sorry.

"Logan, I need to apologize. I was jealous of Akari. I thought you had a crush on her, and it made me act a little bit weird. I hated that we couldn't just do regular things like go to the swimming pool. I'm sorry," she said in a rush before she could change her mind. Once she was finished, she leaned back against the bench, too scared to look at his reaction.

"How can you think I'd rather go to the swimming pool than help stop an evil clown from causing chaos?"

"So…you're not mad?"

"Never," he said before giving her a rueful smile. "Though there was one part of the date I'd been looking forward to." As he spoke, his fingers found hers.

"Oh…" She gulped, but before she could say anything else, he leaned forward and brushed his mouth against hers. *Oh!* She might not be a kissing expert, but as far as she could tell, her first spontaneous kiss was pretty special. Perhaps she wasn't such a regular girl after all.

Acknowledgments

A big shout-out to Sarah Hantz and Christina Philips for seeing me through yet another book!

Also special thanks to Susan Hawk, Wendy McClure, and Eliza Swift. Also to the entire team at Albert Whitman.

To Arthur Holt, who is thankfully a lot better at science and math than I am. Who knew kids could grow up to be plotting buddies? And to Barry and Molly for surviving my interesting deadline cooking.

CATHERINE HOLT was born in Australia but now lives in New Zealand, where she spends her time writing books and working in a library. She has a degree in English and journalism from the University of Queensland and is married with two children. She also writes books for older readers under the name Amanda Ashby and hopes that all this writing won't interfere with her Netflix schedule.

100 Years of

Albert Whitman & Company

1919–2019

Albert Whitman & Company encompasses all ages and reading levels, including board books, picture books, early readers, chapter books, middle grade, and YA

Present

2017
The Boxcar Children celebrates its 75th anniversary and the second Boxcar Children movie, *Surprise Island*, is scheduled to be released

2014
The first Boxcar Children movie is released

2008
John Quattrocchi and employee Pat McPartland buy Albert Whitman & Company, continuing the tradition of keeping it independently owned and operated

1989
Losing Uncle Tim, a book about the AIDS crisis, wins the first-ever Lambda Literary Award in the Children's/YA category

1970
The first Albert Whitman issues book, *How Do I Feel?* by Norma Simon, is published

1956
Three states boycott the company after it publishes *Fun for Chris*, a book about integration

1942
The Boxcar Children is published

1938
Pecos Bill: The Greatest Cowboy of All Time wins a Newbery Honor Award

1919
Albert Whitman & Company is started

Early 1900s
Albert Whitman begins his career in publishing

31901065095640

Celebrate with us in 2019!
Find out more at www.albertwhitman.com.